The CURIOSITY CLUB

Alice Alone

Sally Harris

ILLUSTRATED BY
Janette Hill

Published by

Wacky Bee Books

Shakespeare House, 168 Lavender Hill, London, SW11 5TG, UK

ISBN: 978-1-913292-15-7

First published in the UK, 2022

Text © Sally Harris, 2022

Illustrations © Janette Hill, 2022

Design by David Rose

Printed and bound by Akcent Media

www.wackybeebooks.com

Chapter One

'Can't you just... just... just leave me alone, Alice? Seriously! Go away!'

Gigi stood up and pushed her lunch tray away as she shouted. It slid across the shiny, metal cafeteria table and connected with my lunch box of homemade steamed pork buns. Then the whole lot flipped off the edge of the table and straight down the front of my brand-new school dress.

Piled in my lap was a combination of tomato sauce, meatballs, strands of spaghetti and buns. The sauce coated the front of my checked uniform and dripped down my legs onto my white socks. I leapt to my feet. The meatballs and steamed buns plopped to the ground, one by

one, making a squelching noise on the polished, wooden floor of the cafeteria at St Mildred's.

All of the girls in the cafeteria stopped what they were doing and stared. It was so quiet, you could have heard a pin drop. Or at least a fork drop. In fact, I'm sure I heard a couple of them clatter onto lunch trays. With 450 pairs of eyes upon me, I did what any sensible Year 5 girl would do in this situation.

I ran.

Stares and whispers filled the air as I wove in and out of the packed tables with lunch all down my front.

I was halfway down the corridor before I stopped for breath. I had no idea where I was, let alone where I thought I was going. Where do you even run to when your former best friend tells you to go away and tips her lunch straight into your lap? I could feel my eyes welling up with tears as I replayed everything over and over in my mind.

This was definitely not how I pictured the end of my very first week at St Mildred's.

Everyone kept telling me how much I would love it. At St Mildred's School for Girls, I mean. They said that it was such a great school, with so many opportunities for me there. Their website said they had an art club, a cooking club, chess, gardening and even a synchronised swimming team. You could take extra drama classes or dancing or try out to join one of the many sports teams. It all sounded so exciting, and I couldn't wait to get started.

I wasn't even worried about being the new girl in school. Sure, I know it is usually tough when you're new and you don't know anyone. You have got no one to be your partner in class or to hang out with you at break times or to sit with you at lunch. But I figured that I'd be fine because my best friend was actually coming with me. How lucky is that?

Gigi Burnett and I had been friends since our first day at school five years ago. We just happened to have desks right next to each other, and we bonded quickly over a love of unicorns and a dislike of bananas.

This summer, Gigi had been in France for the whole holidays. Her mother's French, and I think she misses home a lot, so the whole family had gone back there for the summer break. Except in France it's winter, not summer like it is here

in Australia. So, according to Gigi, they'd be spending the whole time with her relatives at a chalet in the mountains, skiing every day and eating baguettes and chocolate croissants when they tired of all that skiing.

I hadn't seen Gigi for a while, so I was looking forward to school starting because we had a lot to catch up on. Neither of us have a phone of our own, so we couldn't even text each other. I'd started keeping a list in a notebook with all the things I'd done since I'd seen her last, like baking a chocolate cake, reading seventeen books and seeing the new *Winnie Mermini: The World's Smallest Mermaid* film at the cinema.

Like I said, I'd been looking forward to my first day at St Mildred's, and it started off pretty normally.

My grandmother, Nai Nai, was already cooking breakfast by the time I came downstairs in my new uniform. She gave me a big smile and pinched my cheeks with her hands.

'You look so grown-up,' she said in Chinese, as she placed a large plate on the table, piled high with fresh dumplings. 'And you're still growing. Eat! Eat!' She pushed the plate towards me, ordering me to eat up.

My little sister, Dorothy, was already at the table. She was wearing a navy blue polo shirt and fleece tracksuit bottoms, just like I used to wear to my old school.

'Exciting day, girls,' said Mum, sweeping through the kitchen and planting a kiss on both of us. She was carrying a large pile of patient files in one hand and reached out to grab a dumpling with the other. Mum's a neurosurgeon. That's a doctor who works on people's brains and their nervous systems, which is how your brain sends messages to different parts of your body.

'Are you going to drop us off at school today?'
I asked, as Mum quickly inhaled her dumpling.

'Sorry, Alice,' she said, wiping her fingers on
the nearest napkin. 'I've got my first patient
booked in at 8 o'clock today, then surgery at 11.
I'm not sure when it'll be finished, so I'll have to
hear all about it when I get home tonight.'

It's funny that even though she's an expert on
brains, Mum sometimes has trouble switching
her own brain off from work. It often feels like
she's either at work or working at home on some
medical case that needs her attention.

As I finished my breakfast, Nai Nai pulled my hair back into two neat plaits, finishing each with a shiny, new, red ribbon to match my uniform. Red is an auspicious colour. It means happiness, joy and good luck to Chinese people. I placed my straw school hat onto my head, then I stood up and twirled around for Nai Nai, showing off my new dress and blazer. I'd even picked out my new glasses in red to match my uniform. Nai Nai smiled and clapped for me.

'Do I look like the perfect St Mildred's girl, Nai Nai?'

Nai Nai shook her head. 'You look exactly like yourself, Alice. What is that thing they say on the Instagrams and the YouTubes? Be yourself – everyone else is already taken?'

I laughed. Nai Nai is terrible with technology, but she always wants us to think she's keeping up.

'No, I think it's that you should always be

yourself,' piped up Dorothy, 'unless you can be a unicorn. Then you should be a unicorn!'

Nai Nai's laughter filled the dining room. She swatted at Dorothy with the dishcloth in her hand. Dorothy dodged and giggled.

'Coffee?' said Nai Nai, holding out Mum's travel cup. Mum grabbed the cup, thanked Nai Nai and was off out the door.

'Now finish up, girls,' ordered Nai Nai. 'Your father said he'll drop you off at school.'

Dad will drop us off?

'I think we'll just take the bus,' I said quickly. 'Or we could walk. We could definitely walk, couldn't we, Dorothy?'

Dorothy, her mouth filled with dumpling, nodded vigorously.

'No need to take the bus or walk,' said my dad as he entered the kitchen. 'I'm here to drive my darling daughters to school on their first day.'

Now, don't get me wrong: we love our dad. He's great! Fantastic! The best! And we love being dropped off at school. It's way easier than having to take public transport, and it's much faster than walking. It's just that his choice of motor vehicle doesn't exactly blend in at school drop-off. Like, at all!

Ten minutes later, Dorothy and I found ourselves buckled into the front seats of Dad's food truck. Dad used to work as a chef in a fancy restaurant in the city. But then the restaurant got sold, and Dad decided that he fancied a change of scene, so he bought himself a food truck. He'd originally planned on selling Chinese food from the truck, but it was all set up for selling Mexican food. Dad decided that it would be a waste to throw out all of that almost new equipment, repaint the truck and start again. So he just changed the sign a

bit, and now it says *Chang's Traditional Chinese Tacos*. I'm not sure what is exactly traditional about selling Chinese-Mexican food, but the crowds seem to love it. It didn't matter where he parked the van; every night there was always a line of customers around the block. The fried rice tacos were a favourite right from the start, and people now come from all over the city to try the seaweed quesadillas, the kung pao nachos and the frozen green tea margaritas. Sometimes I even help, folding napkins and washing dishes, that sort of thing.

'You can probably just drop me off here, Dad,' I said as the truck rumbled up to some traffic lights just before the school. 'I mean, Kent Street is really narrow. You might not be able to turn around or be able to park. I can walk.'

Dad shook his head. 'I've brought you all this way. I'm not going to make you walk now.'

'I really don't mind,' I replied as the truck lurched into Kent Street. The pots and pans in the back of the truck banged and rattled as we sped around.

As we approached the school, I couldn't see a spot for Dad to pull over. There were a lot of parents with their daughters in their fancy cars parked outside the school. Apparently, Dad couldn't see a parking space either because the next thing I knew, he'd turned into the school driveway.

'Dad! I don't think you're meant to drive up

here,' I said, holding on tightly to the door handle as the truck lunged past a welcome sign with a map of the grounds, then flew over a speed hump.

'Nonsense!' said Dad. 'It's a driveway, isn't it? Driveways are for driving on. It's in the name.'

Girls walking up the drive with their school bags leapt aside as the truck rattled by. At the top of the drive was a roundabout in front of the entrance to a large, sandstone building. It had an archway right in the middle and curved turrets at either end. Above the archway was a tower with

a fancy clock whose golden hands glinted in the sunshine.

The food truck growled its way to the top of the driveway, pulled around the roundabout, then came to a stop right outside the archway. All the girls milling around the entrance to the school stopped to stare. Not only was the truck large, noisy and brightly coloured, it was also the only vehicle on the whole driveway. It wasn't exactly the quiet entrance that I'd hoped to make on my first day.

'Thanks for the ride, Dad,' I said quickly. 'See you after school.' I grabbed my school bag, flung open the truck door and jumped down onto the ground.

Unfortunately, this was my first time climbing out of the food truck wearing my new school dress and I hadn't really thought it through. I dropped my school bag down first, then as I slid down from the truck, my dress got hooked on a handle on the edge of the seat. I tripped over and landed with an unceremonious splat on the drive in front of the crowd of waiting girls. I could hear them all gasping, then giggling, even with my face flat on the floor.

Okay, so it wasn't the most perfect start to Year 5, but how was I to know that things were going to get even worse?

Chapter Two

I quickly scrambled to my feet. My cheeks were glowing red as I smoothed down my dress and picked up my school bag. I took a deep breath and flipped my plaits back over my shoulders.

'Love you, Alice,' Dad called loudly. 'Have a great day!' The girls who were still standing around watching laughed again as he revved the truck and hurtled back down the driveway. As I turned towards the large, sandstone arch, something caught my eye. Or rather, someone. Gigi! I saw her curly, blonde ponytail in amongst the group of girls all milling around, staring at Dad's truck.

'Gigi! Gigi!' I shouted, and waved at her. It was a big, enthusiastic whole-arm wave, but she mustn't have seen me, because she turned around and walked through the stone archway and off into the building instead of coming over to say hello.

Engraved in the sandstone over the archway is the school crest, and beneath the crest is the school motto: *Clemens Robur*. It means 'gentle strength', and I love it because it's an oxymoron. Isn't that a great word? *Oxymoron*. It's where two opposite words are used together. Like when someone says that something's pretty ugly. Or bitter sweet. Or an original copy. Or old

news. Or the only choice. You get the idea. And they're the kind of thing that once you know about them, you spot them everywhere. I enjoy spotting oxymorons, and St Mildred's having an oxymoron as a motto was yet another sign that it was the perfect school for me.

I was swept along with the other students through the archway and into the St Mildred's Quadrangle. It had ivy-covered classrooms on all four sides and a huge fountain right in the middle, surrounded by perfectly manicured grass. I could see my reflection in the windows as I walked; I looked like a proper St Mildred's schoolgirl.

Dad says that if Mum had had her way, Dorothy and I would have been St Mildred's schoolgirls from day one of our education, but that he thought it was important that we got to experience co-education first. Co-education is just a fancy way of saying that he wanted us to go to a school with both girls and boys. Anyway, apparently Mum and Dad compromised, and that's why I started at St Mildred's in Year 5 and not at the beginning of primary school.

I miraculously managed to find the Middle School building. The hallways were a surging sea of red – a flurry of students all trying to find their form rooms and lockers. They filled the air with the rattle of combination locks, the thud of books being unpacked and the chatter of girls swapping holiday stories.

My locker was on the second floor, just up the hall from my classroom, and I was proud of myself for only making a few wrong turns to find it. I'd just finished unpacking my bag as a bell rang. I had no idea what that meant, but judging by the fact that most of the girls suddenly seemed to vanish from the hallways into the nearby classrooms, I guessed I was probably meant to be in class by now.

As I snapped my locker door closed, I saw Gigi walking down the corridor towards me. I gave her an excited wave, then promptly knocked off my glasses and dropped my pencil case onto the girl stacking her things into the locker below mine.

'Ouch!' she exclaimed, rubbing her head.

'Oh, my goodness! I'm so sorry!' I said. I fumbled around on the ground for my glasses. 'Are you alright?'

She nodded, picking up my pencil case. 'I think this is yours. Is that Winnie Mermini?' She looked at the picture on the front. 'I love Winnie Mermini!'

I slid my glasses back onto my nose and smiled. 'Me too. Have you seen the new film?'

The girl nodded, and her untidy, blonde hair

swung about enthusiastically. 'Twice! Once with my friend and once with Mum.'

'It was such a good film!'

'So good! Teeny-tiny mermaids are the cutest!' agreed the girl.

'I'm Alice Chang, by the way,' I said. 'And... this is my friend, Gigi.'

Gigi was now close enough to join the conversation. I waved her over. 'You're finally back!' I said to her.

She turned a bit pink. 'Well, I've been back for about a week, but yes, I'm finally back.'

A week? She's been back from France for a whole week and she didn't even call me?

'Gigi, this is...' I trailed off. I was so confused. And I didn't actually know the name of the girl I'd hit with my pencil case.

'I'm Bee,' said the girl, smiling. 'Beatrice O'Connell in all official paperwork, but Bee is just fine. I've been here at St Mildred's since nursery school. And are you a Winnie Mermini fan too, Gigi?'

Gigi wrinkled up her nose. 'No, not really. I've seen some of the earlier films, but I think we're getting too old for Winnie Mermini now we're in Year 5, aren't we?'

What? Gigi loves Winnie Mermini! We've spent hours and hours together discussing her. We've seen all the films together. We've read the books. We've got matching crocheted mermaid tails. We've even got mermaid best friend necklaces that Gigi's mum had bought for us.

A second bell rang, interrupting the awkward silence.

'Should we be going into class now?' I wondered aloud.

Bee nodded. 'I'm in Room 5C. What about you?'

I examined my timetable. 'I'm 5C too,' I said.

Gigi shook her head. 'Not me. I'm 5A. I'm sure I'll see you around though.'

And with that, she disappeared off as quickly as possible through a nearby doorway.

Hang on! Gigi and I aren't in the same class together? But we've *always* been in the same class. I guess that's because there was only one class at our old school. But still, I never thought we wouldn't be in the same class. How will Gigi share her cool pencils that smell like different fruits with me if we aren't in the same class together?

After that, my first morning at St Mildred's passed in a blur. My teacher, Miss Walker, seemed nice enough. When we were all settled in our form room, she had us play some games to introduce ourselves to each other. Then she took us on a tour of the Middle School building. I tried to join in the games and to concentrate when Miss Walker was showing us around, but my mind was only half there. The other half was wondering what was going on with Gigi. How come she hadn't called me when she arrived home? And she doesn't like Winnie Mermini? It felt like she'd gone away to France as one person and come back as someone different.

I couldn't even find Gigi at the first break time. As the bell rang, girls spilled out of every class. After a few minutes, I couldn't even remember who I'd met in my class that morning and who was from a different class. I thought I saw Bee at one point, the girl that I'd dropped my pencil case on, but there were so many more girls at St Mildred's than at my old primary school and they all looked a bit the same in their matching red uniforms. I ended up just hanging out by my locker, pretending that I was organising my books and tidying up an imaginary mess inside.

We did a maths test between break time and lunch, and when the bell rang for lunchtime, I was the first out the door. I would not miss Gigi again. I watched the doorway of 5A carefully, and when the teacher opened it to dismiss the class for lunch, I slammed my locker door shut and bounded over.

It wasn't long before Gigi came out, carrying her books and pencil case under one arm. She was chatting with two girls I hadn't met before.

'Hi, Gigi!' I said.

The two other girls exchanged a look with each other. 'Gigi?' said the taller one. 'Is she talking to you, Georgiana?'

Georgiana? Gigi is only ever called Georgiana by her grandmother. I looked to Gigi to correct her, but she said nothing. Instead, she smiled and said, 'Alice, this is Darcy and Chelsie.' I looked at the two girls standing either side of her. All three of them looked like they were out of a shampoo commercial. Gigi, with her bright blonde curls in a high ponytail, flanked by Darcy on one side, with long, dark hair that was perfectly tousled, and wearing tiny diamond earrings, and Chelsie, on

the other side, with straight, brown hair held back with a red, leather hairband. Their uniforms fit perfectly, like they were tailor-made for them. I felt a bit self-conscious in my slightly too large dress and tugged at the sides trying to smooth it down.

'Alice and I used to go to the same school.' Gigi looked at me awkwardly.

I wanted to add, 'And we're best friends!', but I stopped myself.

'Nice to meet you,' I said to Darcy and Chelsie. I turned back to Gigi. 'So, want to hang out together at lunchtime?' I asked. 'We've got a lot to catch up on. I haven't even shown you all the things I've written in my holiday notebook yet.'

Gigi faltered. 'Maybe. I mean, I guess. I was going to... maybe... just...' She looked at the other two for help.

'We were going to show Georgiana the sights,' said Darcy.

'The hall, then the gymnasium,' said Chelsie.

'Then the swimming pool,' said Darcy.

'Then the theatre,' added Chelsie.

'So we'll definitely be too busy. Sorry about that,' finished Darcy.

The two girls shrugged, like it couldn't be helped that they wanted to walk around and show Gigi all the interesting things St Mildred's had to offer.

'I haven't seen all of those places yet,' I said. I thought they might invite me to go with them.

'You should definitely make sure you see them all some time. We're so lucky that St Mildred's has such amazing facilities,' said Chelsie, sounding like a paragraph from the school website.

I looked at Gigi. 'Maybe we could walk home together tonight then?'

Gigi shook her head. 'I've got dancing after school today.' Then before I could suggest any other days, she added, 'And I've got dancing on Tuesdays and Fridays, piano tomorrow afternoon, and I'm starting at diving club on Thursday.'

'Maybe another time... Alice was it?' said Darcy. She linked her arms through Gigi's, and the three of them headed off along the hallway.

'Hopefully,' I called after them. 'We still haven't discussed the Winnie Mermini film yet.'

Gigi didn't turn around, but I swore I could hear the three of them giggling as they went.

I took my lunch out to the Quad and sat on a bench under the cover of the walkway to eat. It seemed silly to feel lonely when there were 450 other girls right here – walking around the building, running, laughing together, playing games – but I felt very alone. I'd never known school without spending all of my time with Gigi. I didn't know what it looked like without

her. Should I start trying to find someone new?
Maybe that girl who liked Winnie Mermini
might be keen to hang out. Or perhaps, once the
novelty of being at a new school wore off, Gigi
and I could go back to being best friends, just
like before.

Chapter Three

At first, I thought maybe Gigi was just acting weirdly because it was the first day. She'd been so busy with finding her way around St Mildred's and her new timetable and her class that we hadn't really had a chance to catch up. I tried really hard to believe that was true and that it wasn't something more. But every time I saw her after that, she was always too busy to chat, and it kind of seemed like she didn't see me there at all. She snubbed me twice in the library, avoided me after Art and pretty much ran away when I saw her outside the science lab. I tried to catch up with her before school and at break times, but every time I saw her, she was with Darcy or Chelsie. They'd point and whisper and giggle, then walk off together, leaving me alone. I started to get this feeling in my stomach that it wasn't just a bad start, but there was something more going on.

As the week progressed, it also quickly became clear that it wasn't just Gigi that was very different at St Mildred's. The classes were different too. At my old school, our teacher, Mr Sherrin, would usually take us once a week for our PE lesson. It was always a game of football as he used to play professionally before he became a teacher. After some parent complained about the lack of variety, he decided to teach every variation of the game of football that he could come up with – Irish Gaelic football, five-a-side football, three-a-side football, soccer, futsal, and even crab football, which we played scuttling around on our hands and feet and sounded very made up to me.

The next time I got to speak properly to Gigi was at Friday PE. At St Mildred's, all of Year 5 students had their lessons together. This meant that Gigi and I would finally be in the same class. I'd stopped to tie up my trainers on the way to the indoor sports courts when Gigi, Darcy and Chelsie walked past together.

'Hey!' I called. 'Hey, Gi... Georgiana!'

They stopped and looked at me as I ran over to join them.

'So, if we need a partner today for PE, want to be partners?' I asked Gigi.

She looked uncertain. 'I'm not sure that we'll need partners today,' she said. She exchanged a quick look with Darcy and Chelsie. 'But I mean... well, okay, I guess.'

'Thanks,' I said. 'It's hard being new and not knowing anyone, isn't it?'

'Um... right,' said Gigi. I followed her down the steps and onto the court, and we found a spot near Darcy and Chelsie near the back of the group.

There are three types of students in PE lessons. There are the ones who are great at sports, and PE is the best ninety minutes of their week. There are those girls who are not great at sports and for them, PE is the longest, toughest, most nightmarish ninety minutes of their week. Then there is the third category which I like to call 'the invisible middle'. This is the group who aren't good enough to be the stars of every team, and they're not terrible enough for anyone to notice how bad they are either. Or should I say, notice *us*? I'm definitely in the middle group and I'm actually happy with it being that way.

Ms Ports blew her whistle, and everyone snapped to attention.

'Right, girls,' she said. 'Time for today's warm-up. Let's see you running three laps to get us started.'

The entire Year 5 cohort began jogging around the outside of the basketball court. The faster runners sped off, ponytails swinging as they set the pace. At the back, some slower girls started to lag. Some even stopped running, then began to chat and dawdle.

Ms Ports blew her whistle again and pointed to four large bags of volleyballs sitting in the middle of the court. 'Right, we'll practise our skills first in pairs, then we'll play some games in House teams. Everyone choose a partner, grab a ball between two and find a space on the court.'

I turned towards Gigi, excited for us to get to spend some time together, just like we used to do in PE classes back at our old school. We used to laugh so much during our PE lessons together as we tried to master all the skills of the various games of football. We were excellent at passing and kicking by the end, but hopeless at most of the skills needed for any other sport.

Instead, when I turned around to mention this memory to Gigi, I was just in time to see Darcy grab her by the hand. Gigi giggled and followed Darcy over to the bags of volleyballs. On the inside, I wanted to cry and shout and tell her that she'd promised she'd be my partner, but on the outside, I tried not to show how upset I was. Instead, I was filled with panic as everyone else suddenly seemed to have a partner, a ball and a space to throw it in. I was surrounded by volleyballs whizzing back and forth.

Finally, I spotted a girl with bright red hair who looked as lost as I did.

'Partners?' I said as I approached her. She nodded and picked up a volleyball from the bag.

'I'm Cassidy,' she said. 'I'm terrible at volleyball. There, you've been warned!'

Cassidy and I tried passing the ball to each other. She was right. She wasn't great at volleyball. Every time she tried to pass the ball, it would go straight up in the air, straight down into the ground or straight behind her at some wild angle.

Each time she ran off to fetch the ball again, I'd find my gaze wandering off to watch Darcy and Gigi, passing the ball back and forth and laughing together. Then Cassidy would throw me the ball and I'd pass it back to her. Then she'd hit it wildly off somewhere else and run off to chase it again, and I'd start looking for Gigi once more.

'Ready, Alice?' asked Cassidy. I nodded, and she threw the ball to me. I passed it back, and Cassidy passed it back to me again.

Unfortunately, my brain had already decided that she'd miss it again, so I was already looking over at Gigi and Darcy when the ball came whizzing back. To Cassidy's credit, it was an excellent shot, accurate and powerful. The ball hit me square on the side of my face, and I went down like a sack of potatoes.

I heard the girls in the groups near us gasp as I fell over.

'Oh, I've killed her!' I heard Cassidy say. 'I have, haven't I? Oh, my goodness! She's dead, isn't she? I'm sure she is.'

As I lay on the ground, I could feel the world spinning around me, but I didn't feel dead.

Ms Ports came rushing over, whistle jangling around her neck. 'Are you okay?' she asked as she helped me to sit up.

I nodded. The side of my face was tingling from where the ball had smacked me, and my vision was filled with dark spots and lots of tiny stars. At least it had missed my nose, and although my glasses were knocked off, at least they weren't broken.

'Cassidy, help her over to a bench,' said Ms Ports. 'Everyone else, back to the drill, please.' She blew her whistle to show she meant business. 'Now!'

The girls began to walk back to their places. As my vision began to clear, I watched Gigi and Darcy walking together. They were talking and laughing, with Darcy making out like she was falling over in slow motion. It took me a moment to realise that she was pretending to be me. She was holding her fingers up around her eyes to make little circles that looked like glasses, which fell to the floor as she acted out what had happened. After several dramatic re-enactments, she paused to weave her hair into two long plaits. Then she used the plaits as part of her performance, making them wave around dramatically as she pretended to be hit and fall to the ground. Worse than watching Darcy's version of events, however, was seeing Gigi standing there alongside her laughing. Sure, she was laughing at Darcy's acting skills, which were definitely laughable, but she was also laughing at something that had just happened to me. I felt my eyes fill with tears.

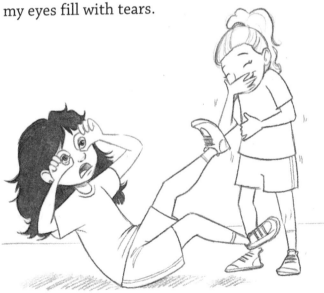

'Are you okay, Alice?' asked Cassidy. 'Do you want me to get Ms Ports again?'

I shook my head. 'I'm fine,' I said, brushing a tear from my cheek. 'It just stings a bit, that's all.'

As I sat there on the bench next to Cassidy, I realised that my answer was true in more ways than one. Sure, my face still stung a bit, but how Gigi was acting towards me possibly stung even more. Possibly what hurt the most was that I could see that we were drifting apart as friends. I knew I shouldn't cling onto her if she didn't want to be my best friend any more, but I didn't know what else to do.

When the bell rang, I was carried along in the stream of girls returning to Middle School. We changed back into our school dresses, and most girls went to their lockers to collect their lunches, while others went straight to the cafeteria, hoping to avoid the lunchtime rush. I grabbed my lunch box from my bag. It was a small, metal canister usually containing some kind of leftover Mexican-Chinese food. I opened the lid. Spiced empanada steamed pork buns. Result!

The tables outside the cafeteria were filling quickly. I spotted Gigi sitting with a plate of spaghetti and meatballs on a tray at the end of a table by herself and seized the moment to try to find out what was going on with our friendship. I slid onto the bench seat opposite her.

'Hi, Gigi... Georgiana... whatever,' I said. She looked up from her plate, expecting someone else. I got straight to the point. 'So what's going on with us?' I asked. 'We're best friends. Or at least, we *were* best friends. But since we arrived at St Mildred's, it's felt like we're total strangers. And, to be honest, I'm feeling very confused about it. What's going on? Why are you acting all... all... different?'

Gigi's cheeks flushed just the slightest bit pink.

'Hello, Alice,' she said. She turned her head one way, then the other, clearly looking for either Darcy or Chelsie to turn up and save her again. They were nowhere in sight. She toyed with her plate of pasta. 'Am I really that different?'

I nodded. 'You're suddenly Georgiana and you're all interested in hairstyling and lip gloss and you say that you don't even like Winnie Mermini any more. I mean, really?'

Gigi shrugged, and she twirled her spaghetti onto her fork. 'Really, Alice. It's not that I don't like Winnie Mermini, it's just that I think it's a bit immature now,' she said. 'I'm allowed to change what I like, aren't I?'

I shook my head. 'It isn't really about that. It's more that –'

'Hello, Georgiana,' said Darcy and Chelsie in unison. 'Oh... hello, Alice. You just seem to be everywhere, don't you?' Chelsie peered into my lunch box. 'Wow! That's an interesting-looking lunch. What is it exactly?'

Great! Darcy and Chelsie. I was in no mood to try to explain my dad's Mexican-Chinese food inventions to them.

'Sorry, but Georgiana and I were trying to have a *private* conversation,' I said. I was feeling frustrated that I still seemed to be getting nowhere with Gigi. I turned away from Darcy and Chelsie.

'I just want to know what's going on, Gigi,' I said quietly, speaking just to her.

'Yeah, *Gigi*,' said Darcy, in a silly high-pitched voice. She emphasised the two syllables of Gigi's name every time she said it. 'Oh, what's going on, *Gigi*? Really, *Gigi*?'

I looked into Gigi's eyes, feeling both helpless and hopeless. She gave away nothing.

Then it was Chelsie's turn to use the same silly voice. 'Want to talk about Winnie Mermini with me, *Gigi*?'

'Want to wear our hair in plaits, *Gigi*?' added Darcy. 'Want to get glasses just like mine, *Gigi*?' They both dissolved into giggles. They might have thought they were being funny, but to me, they were just being mean.

'Come on, Gigi,' I said. 'Let's sit somewhere else.' I reached out and grabbed her hand.

She yanked it out of my grasp.

And that's when it happened.

The great spaghetti, meatballs and pork buns-wearing incident.

Chapter Four

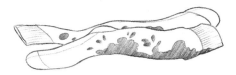

As I stood in the hallway, covered in lunch, and crying, I had no idea what I was going to do and where I was even trying to go. I was completely lost and smelt distinctly of an Italian restaurant. Or rather, an Italian-Mexican-Chinese restaurant.

'Oh, my goodness! Alice!' I turned to see Miss Walker, my form teacher, staring at me. 'What's happened?'

I opened and closed my mouth, but no words came out. She must have thought I was a goldfish, not a Year 5 girl.

'Never mind what's happened,' she said. 'Just come with me.'

She put her arm around my shoulders and

steered me through a maze of hallways, upstairs and down, until we reached a door next to the Middle School Office. It was labelled with a neat, brass sign that said Health Centre. Miss Walker opened the door and ushered me inside.

The woman sitting at a small desk stood up and smiled. 'Who do we have here?' she asked, her eyes looking me over and lingering on the front of my uniform.

'Alice Chang. She's new to St Mildred's this week. She's in Year 5. Alice, this is Mrs Gonzales. She's the school nurse.'

Mrs Gonzales had kind eyes, and cheeks sprinkled with tiny, brown freckles. 'You look like you need to borrow a new school uniform,' she said. Her gaze drifted down to my pasta sauce-splattered legs and feet. 'And perhaps some socks. I think we should be able to clean up your shoes easily enough.'

Miss Walker nodded. 'Sounds perfect. I'll leave you here with Mrs Gonzales then, Alice, and I'll see you back in class after lunch, or whenever you're ready.'

While Mrs Gonzales rummaged around in some cupboards at the back of the Health Centre looking for a replacement school uniform for me, I had a look around. There were four beds in the Health Centre, two on each side of the room. Each had a curtain that could be drawn around it. There was Mrs Gonzales' desk, a couch, a few other chairs and a coffee table. It all looked comfortable, but not so comfortable that you'd want to visit unnecessarily or stay too long.

'Here you go, Alice. These look about your size.' She held up a faded school dress and a pair of socks. She ushered me towards a bed, handed me a plastic bag and pulled the curtain around for privacy. 'Just slip your shoes off first for me, and I'll find something to give them a clean.'

I pulled my shoes off and handed them through a gap in the curtain, then unbuttoned my dress and stepped out of it. I dropped it into the plastic bag with my tomato-stained school socks. Even after I'd taken all the sauce-covered uniform off, I still smelled like garlic, onion, herbs, spices and tomatoes. And pasta. I never even thought pasta had a smell until now. I buttoned up the fresh dress, then sat back on the bed to wait for Mrs Gonzales to return. The uniform was far too big for me, but it was better than walking around smelling like a plate of bolognese.

There was a knock on the Health Centre door, then I heard the door open. I thought it was Mrs Gonzales coming back with my school shoes. I was in no hurry for her to come back. Miss Walker had said I could return to class when I was ready, and I definitely wasn't feeling ready.

'Hello?' said a voice.

I froze. It wasn't Mrs Gonzales.

'Hello? Anyone here?' said the voice.

I cleared my throat. 'Um... hello?'

I heard the Health Centre door close, and the next moment, a face appeared around the edge of the curtain. It was Gigi.

We stared at each other. It was at that moment that I realised that we seemed more like strangers than friends. So much had changed in just a week.

I crossed my arms. 'If you've come to take
a photo of me covered in pasta sauce for your
Instagram, then you're too late. I've already
changed.' I pointed to the uniform Mrs Gonzales
had pulled from the cupboard.

Gigi shook her head. 'I just wanted to come
and say sorry, you know, for the mess.'

'I don't really understand what happened,' I
said, sitting back on the Health Centre bed.

'Well, the tray was more slippery than I thought it was. I didn't mean for it to slide all the way across the table.'

'No, I didn't mean what happened with the tray. I mean, when school finished at the end of last year, we were best friends. Then, what now... we just aren't any more?'

Gigi looked uncomfortable. 'I'm sorry, Alice. In France over the holidays, I just had a chance to hang out with my cousins, and they're into different things. Cooler stuff, like more grown-up. It just made it seem that the stuff we used to like was for babies, you know.'

I fiddled with the edge of the blanket on the bed. 'But I could change. I'm sure I could like the cooler things you like if you just gave me a chance.'

Gigi shook her head. 'You should just like what you like. And... I just... well, I really want...' She seemed a bit embarrassed now and took a deep breath before continuing. 'I actually think I want to have a fresh start here at St Mildred's. An opportunity to reinvent myself to be whoever I want to be... without you.'

I stared at her. I felt like my insides were being crushed. I was suddenly reminded of this girl, Ruth, back at our old school. She pretty much had no friends, but had always been desperate to hang out with us. Gigi always found ways to just brush her off, avoid her and leave her out. This was like that, except that now *I* was Ruth and it didn't feel so great at all.

Gigi was still for a moment. 'Sorry, Alice.'

At that moment, Mrs Gonzales came in with my freshly cleaned shoes and shooed Gigi out. It wasn't until the door closed behind Gigi that I began to cry. Big, wet tears. Definitely embarrassing tears. Mrs Gonzales clearly felt sorry for me because she brought me a glass of water and some tissues and, after I said that I had a headache, she let me stay in the Health Centre for the rest of the afternoon. I'm not even sure what classes I missed while I was in there, but I didn't care. It was the worst day of school ever.

And things didn't get any better when I got home.

As I made my way through the front gate and up the path, I could see Nai Nai standing up on her little, wooden stepladder, wobbling around as she hung red lanterns along the verandah. With all of the dramas at school today, I'd completely forgotten about our special dinner.

Easter is Dorothy's favourite holiday because she loves the thin chocolate of the Easter eggs that you can't find the same at any other time of year. Some kids like Christmas or their birthday the best. But me? My absolutely favourite holiday to celebrate is Chinese New Year. I love the traditions, I love the food and I love the decorations. But after the week I'd had at school, even the thought of our family Chinese New Year dinner didn't cheer me up. I really couldn't have felt less like celebrating.

'Alice! You're home,' Nai Nai smiled. When my grandmother greets you, she's like a puppy. She always bounds right up to you and hugs you enthusiastically. I always expect to see a little puppy dog tail wagging behind her.

'Here, Nai Nai,' I said, dropping my bags by the front door and picking up the remaining lanterns. 'I can do this for you. Do we really need to hang them all up?'

'Yes, of course. We need them all to scare off Nian,' said Nai Nai. Her expression was serious, yet she also gave me a wink. Nian is a lion-like monster who apparently rises from the sea to feast on humans at the Lunar New Year. Legend has it that he's afraid of the colour red, so Chinese people hang the decorations for wealth and good fortune, and to scare off a flesh-eating monster who is afraid of a bit of red and of the noise of firecrackers. I've tried to point out that we aren't in China, and none of our neighbours have any red decorations up. As a result, Nian will have plenty of other people to feast on, so

he'll probably be full before he gets to us, but Nai Nai won't hear of it.

As I was hanging up the lanterns, Nai Nai touched my dress and frowned.

'Alice, where's your uniform? This one isn't yours. Yours is a nice, new one. Not faded, not tired.'

I pointed to the plastic bag by the front door with my spaghetti uniform in it. She peered in. Her brow creased.

'It's a big mess, yes?' she said.

I nodded. 'Yes, a big mess.'

'What happened here, Alice?'

I shook my head. 'I don't really want to talk about it, Nai Nai.'

I hung the last of the decorations and grabbed the two bags. I pulled open the screen door and let it bang shut behind me. After filling the laundry tub with soapy water, I dropped my dirty dress and socks into it to soak. Dad was in the kitchen, preparing food for tonight's feast. He was so busy that I'm pretty sure he didn't even notice me as I grabbed a snack from the pantry and headed up to my bedroom.

I began dragging myself upstairs. All I wanted to do was just flop onto my bed and wallow in self-pity for a while, but...

At that moment, Mum appeared at the bottom of the stairs. 'What's going on with your ruined school uniform, Alice?'

'Alice had a fight at school,' said Dorothy.

Mum raised her eyebrows. 'Is that true, Alice?'

I rolled my eyes and crossed my arms. I wasn't usually like this, but I just couldn't seem to stop myself.

It was unusual for Mum to be home so early. 'Wait – what's going on here?' I said. 'Why are you home?'

'It's Chinese New Year and I wanted to be home early for tonight's dinner.' She kicked off her heels and dropped her bag onto the hall table.

I rolled my eyes. 'Hooray, you're home early for once! One time! Every other day of the year you're busy at work. What about all of the other days when we might need you?'

Then Dad appeared, wiping his hands on a tea towel.

'Alice! That's no way to speak to your mother,' he said.

'Not you as well,' I replied. 'Of course you're conveniently home tonight too. Shouldn't you be off busy inventing a new dish for your food truck or something?'

'Alice!' said both of my parents. Dorothy sniffed loudly and wiped her nose with her sleeve.

'All I'm saying is if you weren't all so busy, then we could have gone to France for the holidays! Then none of this would be happening,' I shouted.

'To France?' Mum and Dad looked confused. 'What does France have to do with anything? None of *what* would be happening?'

'You just have no idea!' I said, then I ran off into my bedroom, threw myself onto the bed and cried.

Chapter Five

It was Nai Nai who was eventually brave enough to venture into my bedroom once things had settled down a bit.

I didn't even have to lift my face from the pillow to know that it was her. I could tell just from the way she sat down on the edge of my bed and stroked my hair.

'Want to tell me what's going on, Alice?' she said. 'Why all the shouting? And what was that about France?'

I rubbed my eyes, which were feeling all scratchy. I'm sure my face was all red and blotchy too.

I shrugged. 'It's complicated, Nai Nai,' I told her.

She shrugged back. 'Try me,' she said. 'You forget that I've been around a very long time, Alice, and I've probably heard it all before.'

So I told her all about my not-so-good start to Year 5 at St Mildred's. I told her about how Gigi had gone to France with her family and had come back all different. I told her everything that had happened with Gigi and her two new best friends. I told her about the big fight at lunchtime.

Nai Nai is an excellent listener. She never interrupts or tells you that you have it all wrong.

Instead, she waited until I was finished, then she sat quietly and thought for a bit, before she spoke.

'When I was a little girl, my mother said to me, "Gold is easy to get, but a close friend is harder to find." And you should never forget that.' Then she gave my hair one final pat before getting up and disappearing out the door.

It was a move that Nai Nai was famous for in our family – giving a mysterious piece of advice, then vanishing, leaving you to try and work out exactly what she meant by it.

I wriggled back and stacked my pillows against the headboard so I could sit up. Surely it's easier to have a friend than to find gold? I mean, if gold was so easy to get, then we'd all be rich. Maybe she meant that gold is very rare and hard to find, and a true friend is even harder to find than that. Was Gigi even my true friend after all? Maybe I hadn't found a true friend yet, but where do you even look to find one? I'd never even really tried to make friends before. My friendship with Gigi just... sort of... happened. I don't even really know how to do it. How do you make friends?

I thought about my options. I could sit in the Quad at break times and hope that someone would come up to me and invite me to join their group. But if nobody ever came, then I'd be sitting there by myself every day. I guess instead I could go up to some groups of girls and invite myself to join them. That could work... or it could seem a bit weird and potentially embarrassing if I was rejected. Plus what if we had nothing in common? Maybe there were lunchtime activities. It might be less awkward talking to girls I didn't know if we had something to do whilst we were talking.

Then it came to me: I could join one of the

many clubs at St Mildred's. Of course! There was such a long list of clubs on the school website. I could just pick one that I liked, and it would be filled with other girls that liked that same thing to become friends with. Perfect!

A whiff of Dad's cooking wafted up the stairs, and it smelled delicious. I swung my legs off the bed and stood up. I was feeling so much better now that I had a plan. My stomach rumbled. I decided to put Gigi and friendships out of my mind for now. Tonight was for feasting. Tomorrow I'd worry about which club to join.

At the end of dinner, Nai Nai produced a small packet of paper. 'Take a piece,' she said as she passed them around to each of us.

'What's this?' asked Dorothy. She held her paper up, and it was so thin that you could almost see right through it to the other side of the room.

'It's wish paper,' said Nai Nai. She handed us each a pen. 'Write a wish for the coming year, then fold it up just like this.' She scrunched the paper gently in her hands, bent it loosely in half, then folded the long edges back on themselves before sliding her fingers inside to pop it out into a little, round cylinder. The little roll of paper could then stand up by itself.

I pulled the lid off my pen, then paused – the inky tip poised just above the paper. What should I wish for the coming year?

I leaned on my leg and wrote my wish onto the tiny square of red paper. It seemed such a stupid thing to wish for, but it was all I could think about. *I want to be popular. I want to have friends.* It's one thing for me to think it on the inside, but it's weird to see my heart's desire written there in front of me in thin, inky letters. I clicked the lid back on my pen and quickly scrunched up my piece of wish paper, then rolled it up, just like Nai Nai had shown us.

'Everyone finished? Come with me.'

We all followed Nai Nai out onto the wooden deck at the back of our house. Going back to school usually also meant the end of summer, but it was still warm outside. The cooling night air was filled with cicada song, and there were a handful of stars sprinkled across the sky.

Nai Nai put a plate down in the centre of the deck and stood her wish paper up in the middle of it. We all copied her, and soon the plate held five small wish paper cylinders. Nai Nai then produced a box of matches from her pocket, lit a match, then gently touched it to the top of each of the papers. At first, they just seemed to be

burning, and I wondered why we had to come outside to watch them. Couldn't we have just set them on fire inside at the kitchen table instead? Then, one by one, as if by magic, the wish papers suddenly lifted off into the sky.

'Wow!' said Dorothy. Her face was alight as each of the wish paper cylinders danced in front of our eyes. 'Wow! Look! That one's mine.' She pointed to the highest one. Even though she was almost too big to be carried these days, she reached for Dad to pick her up so she could get a better look. Nai Nai was wearing a smile from ear to ear as she watched the wishes dance and twirl in the warm, summer night air. I know you're not meant to ask people to tell you what they wished for because that means that it won't come true, but I wondered what Nai Nai's wish was.

As they finished burning, the wish papers returned to Earth as nothing more than charred pieces of ash. I stretched out my hands in an attempt to catch my wish as it fell, trying to hold onto it for a moment longer before the ash gave one final spin and vanished out of sight.

Chapter Six

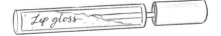

Wouldn't it be nice if that was the end of the story? Or to use one of my favourite oxymorons, wouldn't it have been *awfully good*? Imagine if I could just say that I went to school on Monday and my wish paper had done all the hard work for me and I had girls queuing up waiting to be my best friend. Unfortunately, that was not the case. Instead, I decided that I'd probably have to help my wish along a bit, and so it was that I found myself at the Middle School Office on Monday afternoon. Perhaps Nai Nai was right, and signing up for an after-school club would be the answer.

Over the weekend, while the rest of my family had been relaxing in the afterglow of our New Year celebrations, I'd spent the days browsing the St Mildred's handbook and I'd written down a shortlist of activities that I'd consider signing up for. I figured I'd just talk to the school receptionist and see what I needed to do to get started. It'd be easy and I'd be well on my way to finding a new friend within the week; at least, that's what I told myself over and over. There were actually quite a few options, but I'd narrowed it down to just my favourites. If I was going to commit to a club and go along knowing nobody there, I wanted to choose one that I was really going to like.

There was already a line of students at the reception desk when I arrived at the beginning of lunchtime. The line moved fairly rapidly as the students, one after the other, spoke to a thin, black-haired lady about whatever issue

they seemed to have. The girls seemed to have
a variety of problems that needed solving –
forgotten notices, changes to music lessons, lost
lunch – but the receptionist, Mrs Barry, dealt
with them all in a brisk and efficient manner.

'What can I help you with?' It was my turn.

'I was just wondering if I might be able to sign
up for an after-school club,' I asked, tentatively.

Mrs Barry shook her head. 'The deadline
for sign-ups was two weeks ago. They're fully
booked.' She turned back to her computer. I
just stood there at the desk in a bit of a daze.
Surely, they couldn't be all full? Mrs Barry clicked
vigorously with her mouse.

'Um... so there's really no chance I could join the ice-skating team, the theatre group or the pottery club?'

Mrs Barry turned back to me and nodded. 'The deadline for clubs was two weeks ago. We needed all of the applications back early so we could allocate activities ready for the start of term.' She gave a few extra impatient clicks of her mouse.

'So... they're really all fully booked?'

Mrs Barry nodded. 'Yes, fully booked.' Click, click, click.

What was I going to do now that I couldn't join a club? Just be friendless for ever?

I must have looked pretty pitiful because Mrs Barry then slid a folder out from the shelves next to her and began flipping through the pages.

'There is one club that has space,' she said. She tapped her finger on a blank square at the bottom of a long list of names on one of the pages. My mind began to race with possibilities. Which one would it be? Lacrosse? Drawing? Underwater hockey? I'd take any of them.

'You can have GAS,' she told me.

'Sorry?' I said back. 'I have gas?'

Mrs Barry snorted. 'No, there's room for you to join GAS.'

'I'm sorry... but what is GAS?'

'GAS is short for Girls Achieving in STEM.'

'Achieving in what?'

Mrs Barry looked at me like she thought I might be a bit dim. 'STEM. You know? It stands for Science, Technology, Engineering and Maths.'

'Oh! Okay,' I said. I tried to hide the disappointment in my voice. A group of girls all doing science and maths for fun didn't exactly sound much fun.

'Do you want me to sign you up or not?' Mrs Barry picked up a pen and hovered it over the blank space on the page.

I really wanted to say no. Joining GAS did not sound like the solution to my friendship problem at all. It did not sound like it was going to be my cup of tea. For one  thing, I didn't really know much about STEM. I mean, we'd done bits of it here and there at my old school, but we hadn't had a special science room or anything. We'd just done stuff like putting a white flower in a vase with dyed blue water and watching as the petals turned blue. It was science, sure, but it had never really felt like we'd been doing a proper experiment or investigation. We'd had a few hours on the laptops a couple of times a term, but we'd never done any engineering that I could think of. And who did maths for fun? The idea of a whole after-school club revolving around science, technology, engineering and maths seemed pretty strange to me. It didn't sound like it was going to be very good at all. Was I really going to find my new BFF in a room full of engineering enthusiasts, tech geeks and maths nerds? I highly doubted it. But then again, I hadn't come up with any better ideas, so I might as well give it a go until I could think of something better.

I forced a smile. 'Sure, Mrs Barry. Sounds great. Sign me up!'

And with a final click of her mouse, it was done.

Even though I wasn't particularly excited about attending my first session of GAS, I knew that I had to give it my best shot. What if I went along and everyone was like Gigi and thought that I was really uncool with my long plaits, glasses that matched my school uniform, and a Winnie Mermini pencil case? I'd been thinking about how Gigi had said that coming to St Mildred's was a chance to reinvent herself. She'd changed and had new friends here almost straightaway. If I was going to make friends with the St Mildred's girls, I needed to recreate myself too. I needed a fresh, new look. A cooler image. Gigi had changed and I could too. But how?

The answer to that question came to me when I stopped off to visit Mum at work on my way home the very next day. She usually worked late on a Tuesday night, so I met up with Dorothy at her school and the two of us dropped in to say hello to Mum between her consultations. There are two things that can be relied upon at Mum's surgery: the first is that we'll have to wait to see her and the second is that she always has a great selection of magazines to keep everyone waiting entertained. And that was when I had a great idea.

'Hello, Kristen,' I said, giving Mum's receptionist a wave as we came in. She gave me a wave back.

'Want me to let your mum know that you're here, Alice? I think she has a few more patients to see, but she might be able to fit you in,' she said. Dorothy trotted around behind the reception desk and grabbed the can of fish food. Getting to feed the fish was her favourite part of our visits.

I shook my head. 'That's okay. No need to bother her. I was actually just wondering if I could borrow a few magazines. Do you think it would be alright if I took them home tonight? I'll give them to Mum to bring back in the morning.'

Kristen smiled. 'Be my guest, Alice. I hardly think we're going to notice that a few are missing.'

There are usually about fifty magazines out

in her waiting room, and the receptionists are always swapping them with the latest editions as they arrive in the post, which seems to happen every day.

Whilst Dorothy sprinkled fish food into the tank, I started digging through the various piles

of magazines. I sifted through copies of *Vogue,*
Hot Wheels and *Gardeners' Weekly* until I found
what I was looking for: the teen magazines. I
pulled about six from the stack and stuffed them
into my school bag.

Kristen was on the phone when we went to
leave, so I just gave her a wave and mouthed,
'Thank you!' She gave me a thumbs up as we
nipped out the door and headed home.

As soon as I arrived home, I spread the
magazines out on my bed. They were a rainbow
of bright colours – clashing hot pinks and reds,
neon citrus and cornflower blue. Each of the
magazines had a teenage girl on the cover. They
all looked very similar to each other – a pretty
girl with impossibly perfect skin, hair and teeth.
Actually, the girls reminded me a bit of Darcy and
Chelsie. All of the magazines promised a host of

things, including how to perfect your ponytail. Twenty-six ways to get ready for winter, how to turn up your confidence, unbelievably good gift ideas and a guide on getting great skin in a week. The one that promised you how to become *seriously funny* was my personal favourite, because it had an oxymoron in it. Looking through the magazines, hardly any of the girls looked like me. They weren't Chinese for a start, and none of them were wearing plaits or glasses or a sensible-looking school uniform.

I grabbed a notepad and started writing down ideas as I flipped through the pages. Soon I had a list full of ways to give myself a makeover of sorts. The ideas were nothing major. I couldn't dye my hair blonde, for example, like some of the girls in the magazines, or Mum, Dad and Nai Nai would all go completely nuts. But perhaps I could try a perfect ponytail instead. I'd never have cute

dimples when I smiled, but I could take some of
the money from my savings and buy a tube of lip
gloss to have shiny lips like the magazine girls.
There wasn't much I could change about my neat
school uniform, but my matching glasses would
have to go. I could act cool and confident, just
like the magazine girls said.

When the bell rang for the end of school on
Thursday, I lingered at my locker until all of
the girls from 5C had left. Then, when nobody
was watching, I pulled out the hair ties and
ribbons from the ends of my plaits and shook
out my hair before tying it into a messy, high
ponytail, just like the magazines had suggested.
I wiped the tube of cherry lip gloss I'd bought at
the pharmacy across my lips, then took off my
glasses. My vision was pretty far from perfect,
but I could see just enough to get by for an hour-

long club. I tucked the ribbons and glasses into my blazer and shoved it into my school bag. I wasn't sure that I was going to find new friends at GAS, but hopefully now I at least looked like someone that the girls at St Mildred's might want to be friends with. I swung my bag over one shoulder, took a deep breath and headed down to the Learning Lab.

Chapter Seven

I thought the Learning Lab would be full of girls sitting at desks, reading textbooks and answering questions in their notebooks, but it was the exact opposite. The room was full of movement and energy and laughter. There were about twenty girls from all different year levels and they were all busy. Some were folding paper, some were fiddling with iPads and robots, and others were just standing around chatting, blazer sleeves rolled up, waiting for things to kick off. I sidled in and stood awkwardly at the edge of the room. On the inside, I was feeling so many feelings – excited, nervous, thrilled, worried, shy – all at once. But on the outside, I tried to show none of these things. Instead, I focused on keeping up a cool, popular girl exterior.

'Remember, Alice,' I told myself. 'The goal is to be cool and make friends.'

A tiny, energetic teacher appeared at the front of the room. She was wearing a navy, striped jumper, a bright pink skirt and these beautiful, gold high heels with a large buckle on the side. More eye-catching, though, were her glitter glasses frames that caught the light, and the huge smile on her face. In an instant, the girls stopped talking and fiddling with things and looked at her with interest. 'It's Dr Mathers!' exclaimed one of the girls.

'Yes! Dr Mathers! I was hoping she'd be running the group again this year,' said another.

'Welcome back, girls,' said the teacher. 'I hope you're all looking forward to another year of hard work here at GAS.'

The girls laughed. 'Bring it on, Doc!' one of the older girls called out.

'We can handle it!' The others laughed again.

'Okay, Melody. I *will* bring it on, so to speak,'

Dr Mathers smiled. 'Let's get right to work. At the end of this term in GAS, we're going to be entering a big competition called the Think League Challenge.' Dr Mathers connected her iPad to the projector to display a bright pink screen, and one of the older girls dimmed the lights.

'The Think League is a group that runs science, maths, engineering and technology activities for girls, and this year it's hosting a challenge where schools can send along teams to compete.'

I sneaked a look around at the other girls in the room. Everyone was hanging on every word Dr Mathers had to say, completely enthralled.

'Now, I'd love to be able to take all of you to the competition, but we can only take along three teams of three girls. I've decided that the fairest way to choose which girls get to represent us in the competition is to have a little competition of our own. You'll be working with a randomly assigned group of three and they'll be your group for the whole term. Each week, I'll give you a different STEM challenge to complete. The three teams that do the best in these challenges will then get to go to the Think League Challenge as our official representatives. Got it?'

'Got it!' the girls chanted back together.

Their energy was infectious. I found myself torn between wanting to appear cool and wanting to join them. I managed to hold myself back.

'Now, today's challenge is called The Marshmallow Tower. Can I get an excited *Ooooooooh*, please, girls?'

All of the girls in the room suddenly said 'Ooooooooh!' at the same time, like a marshmallow tower was the most exciting thing they'd ever heard of. I squinted to try and read the information Dr Mathers had displayed on the screen.

'You have thirty minutes to complete today's challenge, and each group will be given a bag containing a wooden board, a hundred mini marshmallows and seventy-five toothpicks. Your mission is to construct the tallest tower that you can out of the equipment. Your tower needs to be able to be transported to the table right here at the front of the room from wherever you build it on the wooden board. Also, it must be both the tallest and able to stand completely by itself for fifteen seconds in order to win. Got it?'

'Got it!' shouted back the girls again.

Melody raised her hand. 'So... like... what happens if we happen to accidentally eat some of the marshmallows?'

Dr Mathers shrugged. 'You eat as many as you wish, Melody. However, I haven't brought along any replacements, so you'll be compromising the height of your tower if you do.'

Dr Mathers flicked to the next slide where she had listed everyone's names in groups of three. There was a flurry of movement and voices as the girls skimmed the list looking for their names. I hung back, unable to read the small print on the screen and fully aware that even if I found the names of the girls in my group, I'd have no idea who I was then looking for.

Next minute, I heard a loud voice over the top of all of the hubbub. 'Alice Chang? I'm with Alice Chang. I don't even know who that is.' When I saw where the voice was coming from, I found it hard to believe that so much noise was coming from such a tiny girl. She had shiny, dark eyes, very curly, dark hair, and it seemed like she had a

lot of attitude and personality.

'Cleo, I think that's her over there.' Bee pointed in my direction. The small girl turned to look at me with her hands on her hips. She looked me up and down.

I smiled and gave a little wave. 'That's me,' I said, trying to sound cool and sophisticated. 'I'm Alice Chang.'

'I'm Cleo. And I know that I look like I should be in Junior School, but I'm actually in Year 5,' Cleo said, as she upended the bag of supplies onto the table. Dozens of marshmallows and toothpicks poured out. 'You look new. Are you new?'

I nodded. 'Yes, I'm in Year 5. Second week at St Mildred's. I think Bee and I have already met. She's in my form class.'

Bee nodded. 'I remember meeting you and your pencil case on the first day.'

I blushed and nodded. 'Don't worry. That pencil case no longer comes to school.' After Gigi had made fun of it, I packed my stationery into a plain, metal pencil tin and hid my Winnie Mermini pencil case away under my bed. I fiddled with the mermaid friendship necklace from Gigi around my neck, running it back and forth along the chain between my fingers.

Bee smiled. 'It's okay. I didn't mind the Winnie Mermini pencil case, even if it did feel like it was filled with lead weights.' She dramatically rubbed her head on the spot where it had hit her. 'And how have you been enjoying St Mildred's so far? It's the best, right? Isn't it the best?'

I wanted both Cleo and Bee to think I was cool, so I tried to think about what Gigi and her new friends would be like if they were here.

'I guess it's okay,' I said, shrugging and trying to seem disinterested and unimpressed.

Both Bee and Cleo seemed a bit disappointed by my unenthusiastic response.

'Well then... Alice-in-your-second-week-at-St-Mildred's, have you got any ideas about how to tackle this challenge?'

I shook my head. 'I've only ever used marshmallows for eating before now. I've never built anything with them.'

Bee smiled. 'Same with me. But last year in GAS, we did a few construction challenges and one thing I remember is that triangles are the strongest shape we could use. I think we should use the toothpicks and marshmallows in groups of three to make triangles to make our tower. Like this.' She picked up a toothpick and stuck each end into one of the mini marshmallows. Then she added two more toothpicks into the marshmallows and joined them with a third marshmallow to create a triangle. 'See?' she said. 'Now I think we make lots of these, all joined to each other.'

Cleo nodded. 'And we just have to remember to make sure we're building up to get a tall structure, not just one with a wide base.'

I got to work making triangles and passing them to Cleo and Bee, who began joining them together using some of the other toothpicks to make our tower.

'So why are triangles the strongest shape?' I asked.

'It's because when you put force on them, it's spread out between all three sides. The angles where the sides meet in the corners are strong and when you put pressure on a triangle, it can't change into any other shape. Think about a square. If you push down on the top of it, it could just slide to the side and become a rhombus.' Bee picked up four toothpicks and some marshmallows and deftly turned them into a square. 'Look,' she said, standing the square up on its edge and pushing down on the top of it. The square immediately folded flat to one side.

'Now, triangles are so strong that they're used in heaps of buildings and bridges and things like that. Now that you know about them, you'll see them everywhere.' Bee pushed down on top of one of the triangles she'd made. The toothpicks held strong, even with the downwards pressure. I was impressed and wanted to ask more questions, but I didn't want to seem too interested. Instead, I just nodded, then pretended to be more interested in my fingernails instead.

There was a hum in the room created by all the groups chatting away quietly to each other as they worked. It was loud enough to share their ideas, but quiet enough for the other girls to not be able to overhear them. When I looked around, I could see quite a few other groups also using triangles in their designs, although some groups were trying some totally different ideas. One group was making long rows of toothpicks and marshmallows, and I wondered how they'd get them to stand straight up in the air for fifteen seconds when they were done. Another team was creating cubes out of toothpicks and marshmallows, then carefully stacking them on top of each other.

'What do you think?' asked Cleo. I looked up from examining my fingernails and squinted to see our tower clearly. It was definitely taking shape. Bee and Cleo had expertly connected all the triangles into a neat, stable tower. I looked around the room. It was close to being the tallest tower and it seemed to be definitely one of the most stable. I stuck our final few marshmallows onto the ends of toothpicks and passed them to Bee. She carefully added them to the top layers of the tower. Bee and Cleo stepped back to admire their work.

'Looks good, I guess,' I said, trying to maintain my super cool appearance.

Cleo turned and rolled her eyes at me. 'I think you mean that it looks *amazing*, Alice. It's a great tower.'

Bee nodded. 'It's definitely a great tower. We are totally going to win. That means maximum points and *that* means maximum chance of getting to go to the Think League Challenge. And I really, really want to go. All three of my brothers have been and they won't stop going on about how good it was. I want to see it for myself.'

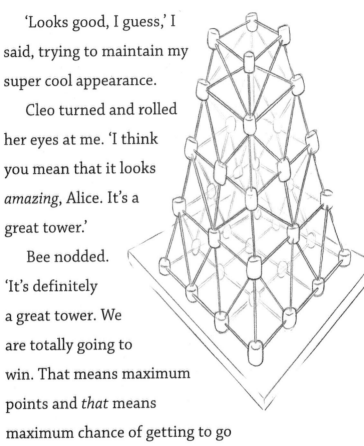

The conversation was interrupted by a musical beeping noise. The timer Dr Mathers had set on the whiteboard was going off.  Our tower-building time was up.

'Right, everyone,' Dr Mathers clapped her hands to get our attention. 'Please put down your toothpicks and marshmallows and step away from your work. That's you too, Melody. Yes, I can see you. Please put down the marshmallows. No, not in your mouth! Girls, it's time to measure the towers and see which one is the tallest. Everyone leave your towers, grab a folding chair and come down and sit around the table I've set up at the front of the room. Then, one by one, you'll be able to carry your tower up to the front for the judging. Don't forget, you'll get points for stability and for height.'

When everyone was settled, Dr Mathers
called the first group up with their work. Three
of the older girls got up, and two of them carried
their tower to the front. It was taller than ours,
but much less stable. Although they were able to
carry it carefully between two of them, it wasn't
able to stand by itself for fifteen seconds, so they
were eliminated. The rest of the girls clapped
and cheered them for their effort. Other groups
followed; some were more successful than others.
The group that had gone for the long chains of
marshmallows and toothpicks were unable to get
their tower to stand. The group that had made
cubes had a fairly stable tower, but it wasn't
very tall because each of the cubes used up quite
a lot of the materials. Most of the towers were
successful in some way, whether it was the height
or how sturdy it was or even just how well the
girls had worked together. Dr Mathers was really

good at pointing out the positive things about each group. No wonder all of the girls loved her running the GAS sessions.

Finally, it was our turn. We'd decided that I'd carry the board with the tower carefully up to the table, and Cleo and Bee would walk alongside me, ready to catch the tower if it fell. This probably wasn't the best arrangement, considering I couldn't exactly see clearly without my glasses, but I didn't want to tell Bee and Cleo that.

'That looks so good,' called out one of the Year 8 girls.

Bee smiled, and we walked up to the front carefully. I was taking tiny steps, holding the board tightly between my hands and using my forearms to steady it. We were almost at the table at the front when it happened. With hindsight, we probably should have seen it coming. Because I couldn't really see very well without my glasses, and with strands of my hair hanging out of my ponytail in my face, I walked a bit too close to the folding chairs near the front of the room. The toe of my school shoe got hooked on one of the chair legs. It was just the toe of my shoe. Just the teensiest tip of my shoe, really. The result, however, was not just a little trip over. You know where you might trip, but can scramble around a bit and find your feet again. No, that wasn't what happened. This was an almighty tumble. I'm sure I actually flew through the air and crashed straight into Cleo, who bumped into Bee. Of course, with all of this flailing around, our tower was flung straight up into the air.

Everyone in the room let out a gasp as the tower took flight. Everything was suddenly moving in slow motion, a carefully choreographed battle of toothpicks and marshmallows in mid-air, like dozens of tiny,

pink and white ninjas fighting each other with sticks. As Cleo, Bee and I lay on the Learning Lab floor where we'd fallen, marshmallows and toothpicks rained down all around us. We sat up, peppered with the pieces of what was once a magnificent tower.

The other girls were actually very nice about it. They all jumped up to help gather all of the pieces and said nice things like 'What a shame!' and 'Your tower was totally going to win!' and 'Oh, that was such a good design too!' Bee and Cleo's friends hugged them and patted them on the back to reassure them that it was just bad luck. I could tell that they were really disappointed though. Someone eventually helped me to my feet and pointed out that there were toothpicks and marshmallows in my hair. I just tried to shrug it off, like I was far too cool to care too much about something as simple as a

toothpick tower and having mini marshmallows toothpicked into my hair. But on the inside, I felt more than a little crushed.

When Dr Mathers wrote up the scores onto her big whiteboard, Cleo, Bee and I ended up getting the average score of all the groups. We scored five out of ten because whilst our tower was tall and strong, it hadn't been officially judged like the others had been. It wasn't a terrible score, but it still felt like I'd lost at tower-building and at friendship-building.

Chapter Eight

I seriously considered never going back to GAS again. I mean, wouldn't you?

Despite my best efforts at trying to act like Gigi, all older and cooler and more sophisticated, I hadn't exactly made myself the most popular girl in the room. Especially not after I'd tripped over and ruined the tower. My cheeks still went red when I thought back on it, even days afterwards. At first, I'd decided that I was going to quit the group altogether, but then I realised that if I was going to make friends at GAS, I was probably going to have to think more like a scientist. A scientist would never try something once and then just give up. No way! Instead, they'd keep trying their ideas until they eventually solved the problem. So that's what I decided to do, and I couldn't just give up after just trying GAS once. Instead, I was going to keep working on developing my new image and trying to act just like the popular girls, just like a scientist would work on perfecting their latest experiment.

I stopped wearing my glasses to school altogether, tucking them into a side pocket in my school bag as soon as I got there. Changing my hairstyle was a bit harder, as Nai Nai had always done my hair for me. I didn't want to hurt her feelings, so I still let her plait it for me while I ate my breakfast, then I pulled it all undone as I walked through the archway to start my day at St Mildred's. When I got home in the afternoon with a loose ponytail instead of plaits, I just told her that they'd fallen out or I'd had to change them for a particular subject like drama or swimming or PE. I still had the mermaid necklace from Gigi around my neck. It was like the last little piece of the old Alice.

When I walked into my next session of GAS the following week, I was feeling like I was really getting into the swing of acting like the new and improved version of myself. The new Alice. I hadn't just changed my hair and glasses. I was even trying to answer fewer questions in class so the other girls wouldn't think I was a nerd or a know-it-all. I was so busy trying to act like the new version of myself that I hardly had time to miss Gigi. Okay, so that part isn't exactly true. I missed my friendship with Gigi a lot, and seeing her smiling and laughing and hanging out with Darcy and Chelsie really hurt my feelings, especially as I was still hanging out by myself. But that was going to change, I reminded myself.

Just as soon as the other girls got to know the new, cooler Alice, I'd be laughing, smiling and hanging out with friends in no time.

Instead of bags of toothpicks and marshmallows at the front of the room this week, Dr Mathers had the Learning Lab set up with jars. Lots and lots of jars. They were all different shapes and sizes; some were tiny and some were tall. They were all filled with different liquids. There were some that looked familiar, like honey, water and oil, and others I wasn't so sure about.

The room was filled with chatter about what today's challenge might be. The scores from last week's challenge were still up on the wall for everyone to see. There was still plenty of time for Bee, Cleo and me to get a great overall score. Most of the teams weren't too far ahead of us as they hadn't scored highly for the stability or height of their tower.

'Are you ready for today's challenge?' said Dr Mathers, appearing wearing a polka-dot jumper and bright green tassel earrings. She held her hand in the air to get our attention. The room went silent. Dr Mathers picked up a jar from the table in front of her.

Filled almost to the top with a rainbow of liquids, the jar was beautiful. Many of the girls were so amazed that they actually let out little gasps of astonishment. Inside the jar were brightly-coloured layers that each caught the light. There were layers in red, orange, green, blue and purple. You'd think that they'd all mix together to make brown, but they didn't. Instead, they were all sitting neatly on top of one another.

'Today's challenge is to create a rainbow in a jar,' said Dr Mathers, her glitter glasses twinkling. 'For each group, there's food colouring, honey, blue washing-up liquid, water, olive oil, surgical spirit and a whole lot of jars and spoons for mixing. Your group has forty minutes

to create your own rainbow jar, just like mine up here. Send someone up to collect your tub of equipment, choose a table and get started.'

Bee picked up the tub of equipment, and I chose some stools at a bench running along the edge of the room. Cleo went to take a closer look at Dr Mathers' rainbow jar.

She came back almost breathless. 'It must be science, but it seems like magic. The coloured layers really are just sitting there on top of each other! How did she do it?'

We stared at the tall, empty jar, then at the containers of liquid and food colouring in front of us. Cleo picked a random curl from her hair and began twisting it vigorously between her fingers.

'So... like... where do you think we should start?' I said, trying to sound cool and not too interested in the activity, even though I was as impressed with Dr Mathers' rainbow jar as Cleo was. I flicked my ponytail over my shoulder in what I hoped was a sophisticated way.

Cleo rolled her eyes. 'So... like... I have no idea,' she replied, imitating me exactly, right down to the hair flick. Whilst Bee seemed to have accepted me into the group, it was clear that Cleo was going to take more convincing. It was like she could see through my pretend cool girl personality.

Bee elbowed her. 'Perhaps we should see what happens if we combine some of the different liquids in a small jar first. She reached out, grabbed the bottle of water and tipped a little bit into a jar. Then she dropped some of the washing-up liquid in on top. The washing-up liquid sank to the bottom of the jar, sitting underneath the water.

'Should I stir it?' asked Bee, holding the jar up to the light. Cleo immediately shook her head.

'I don't think so. Otherwise it'll start to foam

and go all bubbly, just like it does when you mix it with the water to do the dishes. Dr Mathers' rainbow is definitely not bubbly!'

Next, Bee took another of the small jars and added some of the water and the surgical spirit. Because they were both clear liquids, it was impossible for us to tell what they were doing in the jar together. So Bee tried it again for a second time with a few drops of green food colouring in the surgical spirit. This time, it was clear that the green surgical spirit was happy to sit on top

of the water. In a third jar, Cleo splashed in some water and dropped in some of the olive oil. The oil droplets twirled and bobbed on top of the water. It reminded me of washing the dishes for Dad in the food truck. There was always plenty of oil on the pans that he used to make his Chinese-Mexican food, and by the time I'd finished washing up and pulled out the plug, the water always had a layer of oil sitting on the top. Dad said that happens because the oil is less dense than water, so it can sit on top of it.

'That's it!' I said loudly, forgetting all about trying to be cool. 'Of course! That's how she made the layers.'

'What's *it*?' said Bee. She seemed surprised to hear excitement in my voice.

'So it's like the oil and the water in my family foo...' I stopped myself just in time before I could say *food truck*. Nobody wants to be friends with someone who spends half their spare time washing dirty frying pans.

'I mean... in my family, when we go out to, like, a fancy restaurant and they have those bottles of olive oil and balsamic vinegar on the table for you to dip your bread in. And when you pour them onto your plate, they don't really mix. The balsamic vinegar just sits on top of the olive oil because it's less dense.'

Bee and Cleo just stared at me. They looked a bit confused.

Dr Mathers, who'd been walking around to see what each of the groups was up to, stopped by our group to listen in on our conversation. I was a bit nervous explaining my idea in front of Dr Mathers.

'So the liquids we've been given are different densities, which means some will sink and others will float,' I explained. 'If we carefully add them to the jar in the correct order, then they'll all sit on top of each other in layers.'

Dr Mathers gave me the tiniest of nods.

'Are we on the right track, then?' I asked her.

She smiled again. 'I can't tell you that as it wouldn't be fair to the other teams. What I can say is that I really like your thinking, Alice. You explained your idea really well, and I can't wait to see what happens when you test it out.' Then she turned on her sparkly, green ballet flats and walked off to look at what the other groups were up to.

Cleo looked at the tests in the small jars that we'd already made and nodded. 'I do actually think you're onto something, Alice. And once we've worked out the order of the liquids from most dense to least dense, we'll be able to add food colouring to the liquids so that when they're layered...'

'...they'll make a rainbow!' Bee finished.

Cleo pushed up her sleeves and grabbed her pencil. She drew the tall jar on a piece of paper and divided it into five layers. 'Right! It's time to get to work. We already know that the oil will sit on water, and seeing as the oil is naturally yellow, I think that it must make the orangey yellow section of the rainbow. And we know that the surgical spirit is less dense than the water too, so I bet it'll sit on top of the oil as well. Let's make that red.'

'The washing-up liquid is blue, and we know that sank to the bottom of the water,' said Bee.

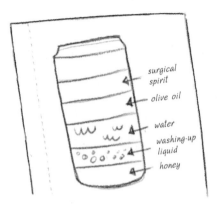

surgical spirit
olive oil
water
washing-up liquid
honey

'That means the water is probably the green layer.'

'Which just leaves making purple honey for the layer at the bottom,' said Cleo.

We stared at Cleo's diagram with each section labelled. It suddenly seemed too easy. 'Should we try it?' I asked. The other two nodded vigorously and we got to work.

I mixed up the different liquids with the right food dyes, and Bee held the jar while Cleo carefully poured in each layer. We watched as each liquid slowly ran down the inside of the jar and settled on top of the ones before it.

'I can't watch,' said Bee, as Cleo picked up the red surgical spirit I'd prepared – the final layer of our rainbow. All of the others were sitting on top of each other perfectly. 'What if it's wrong?' said Bee, her eyes squeezed shut. I realised that I was holding my breath in anticipation.

'It's not wrong. I'm sure of it,' said Cleo. She expertly poured the surgical spirit into the jar where it sat as the top layer of our rainbow.

'Yes!' cheered Bee. The liquids in the jar swayed dangerously, and Bee quickly put the jar down onto the bench so she wouldn't mix up the layers with her enthusiastic celebration.

'That was such a great idea of yours, Alice.' Bee smiled at me, and I couldn't help but smile back. It was a smile that reminded me a bit of spending time with Gigi, back when it was just fun and easy to be friends. I felt myself relaxing, letting my guard down and allowed myself to be my old self. Just for a moment I forgot about having to be the new Alice, the cool girl Alice.

'Should I take it up to show Dr Mathers?' I said, reaching for the jar. I was so excited that my idea had worked and I really wanted to show her.

Quick as a flash, Cleo put out her hand to stop me. 'I don't think you should be the one to carry it, Alice,' she said pointedly. 'Not after last time we let you carry something! You might trip over again and it'll be smashed to smithereens.'

I felt my cheeks turning red, and I pulled my hand back away from the jar like I'd just touched something hot. Immediately, that comfortable, relaxed feeling that I'd been starting to feel with Bee and Cleo was gone.

'Cleo!' said Bee, in a scolding tone. 'That was just an accident. I'm sure Alice will be extra super careful this time around, won't you, Alice? And it was because of her idea that we were able to make the layers like this.' She stared into the jar with its glistening rainbow layers sitting carefully on top of each other. 'But then again, perhaps I should just carry it, Alice? I mean, it's just so pretty. I'd hate for something to happen to it.'

I shrugged. 'It's fine. I mean, whatever. I don't really care. It's just a silly old jar of liquids.' Actually, I did care about it. Deep down, I wanted Dr Mathers to be impressed with our jar and that my idea had worked. I was just feeling cross with myself for relaxing and letting Bee and Cleo see through the new image I'd been working so hard to create.

'Wow! Girls! You did it. Great effort. Are you proud of yourselves?' Dr Mathers exclaimed when Bee carried the jar up to show her our work. Bee and Cleo both nodded and I just sort of stood there. I felt like I wasn't really part of the group any more. I pulled my tube of lip gloss from my pocket and swiped it across my lips.

'Are you pleased with the result, Alice?' Dr Mathers asked me, after she'd finished admiring our jar.

I nodded, trying to contain my excitement that it had actually worked and play it cool. 'I mean, I think it's okay.'

It turned out that we were the only team to create a rainbow in our jar that was exactly like hers. Only one other group came close, but they had accidentally turned all of their washing-up liquid brown, which meant the colours of their rainbow weren't quite right. As a result, we got a ridiculous number of points, which took us from somewhere lost in the middle of the pack, to almost the top of the scoreboard. There was just one other team ahead of us.

Bee and Cleo were both beaming with happiness. They jumped up and cheered when our score was announced. Deep down, I wanted to jump up and celebrate with Bee and Cleo too, but that kind of behaviour didn't really fit with who I was trying to be as cool Alice. I couldn't imagine Gigi and her new friends jumping around after solving a science puzzle. Instead, I just hung back.

Then Cleo turned around and offered me her hand for a high five.

Before I could really think about it, my arm was in the air and our hands slapped together. Cleo's curls bounced around as we connected and she smiled. It was like we'd finally connected with one another. And, despite my best efforts to remain cool, I couldn't help but give just a little smile back.

Chapter Nine

After the success with the rainbow jar, I felt like things began looking up for me at St Mildred's. For one thing, I'd almost perfected my new personality. I was no longer the nerd with plaited hair and glasses who put her hand up to answer every question. Instead, I was sitting back, pretending to be more interested in lip gloss, magazines and boy bands than I was in learning. It was also kind of annoying not being able to see properly, but I felt like it was a small price to pay to feel like I might fit in with the other girls.

At our GAS sessions, Bee, Cleo and I also had some really successful challenges that scored us a lot of points. In one of these, we had to create a lolly stick catapult to launch a small, plastic

army man as far as we could. Bee was super helpful in that one because apparently her three older brothers used to leave those army men all over the house, so she had plenty of experience experimenting with them at home. Our army man flew the furthest of all of the groups and we scored well.

We also did pretty well on the egg drop, where we could use balloons, plastic straws, cardboard and tape to protect an egg as we dropped it off one of the balconies at school. Cleo had the great idea that we should cut the balloons up and use them more like rubber bands. We used them to suspend the egg, so it hung in the middle of a box. When the box hit the ground, the egg was safe because the strips of balloon absorbed the energy.

Of course, we had a couple of challenges that didn't go perfectly too. We had to design a car made from a plastic bottle on wheels which was powered by air released from a  balloon on the top. Our car drove for a long time; the only problem was that it drove around in circles instead of going the furthest distance in a straight line. Another failure was our sinking ship. We were meant to be building a boat out of aluminium foil and cardboard that could hold as many one-dollar coins as possible. Dr Mathers put them in, one at a time. It only took three coins for our ship to sink to the bottom of the tray of water, whilst some groups were able to get theirs to hold the weight of over ten coins.

Despite all of the ups and downs of our GAS sessions, the most important thing to come out of them was that I felt like Bee and Cleo were starting to like me. Or at least they were starting to like this new version of me. Either way, we worked together well during our GAS sessions and enjoyed trying to solve the problems set by Dr Mathers together. And, we were still in amongst the top teams in the running to be chosen for the Think League Challenge. We were currently sitting in fifth spot, which meant that we had to do really well on the final task and get enough points to move into the top three. This was going to be tricky because the four teams above us were all made up of older girls who'd had a lot more experience at GAS than we had.

You could definitely feel a buzz in the air when Dr Mathers arrived for our final session.

'Today is our last task that will enable you to score points which will then decide which teams are going to make it through to represent us at the Think League Challenge,' Dr Mathers announced once everyone had settled down. 'However, there are quite a few teams that are in close contention to be selected, so I've decided to make this final challenge even more... well, even more challenging.' We all laughed, and Dr Mathers joined us. 'It's going to be spread over two sessions of GAS. This week and next week. I'm also going to open the Learning Lab up on Monday at lunch break for any teams that would like some additional time to work on their designs.'

'This must be going to be a *big* challenge,' murmured Bee, under her breath. She tucked some strands of her hair back behind her ears.

'Allow me to introduce you to the Marble Run task,' said Dr Mathers, and she tapped the screen in front of her. The lights in the room dimmed and her presentation appeared on the screen. 'Your job is to create a marble run using cardboard, scissors, glue and masking tape. It should take exactly eight seconds for your marble to get from the top to the bottom.'

'That's it?' said Melody. 'Just a marble run?'

Dr Mathers smiled. 'Yes, Melody. Just a very, very precisely timed marble run. Anyone can make one, but can you make it so that it runs exactly to time, every time? Every millisecond under or over will deduct points from your final score.'

'That's a bit harsh, Doc,' said one of the other Year 8 girls.

Dr Mathers nodded. 'It's *very* harsh. But I can't send you all to the Think League competition, so I have to have a way of awarding points to decide the winning teams. Now, there are scissors and tape here up the front, as well as quite a few cardboard boxes that I rescued from the Staff Room recycling. There's enough for you to get started, but you might want to raid your own recycling at home to find some more empty boxes to work with. There are also stopwatches up the front here to help with your precise timing. Good luck, girls!'

There was a flurry of movement as girls grabbed tape, cardboard and scissors and moved to various corners of the room with their groups to begin work on their design.

Sitting at what had become our favourite table, Cleo was quick to pull out her notepad and pencil. 'Right, any ideas?' she said.

Bee shook her head. 'I haven't built anything like this before and all I can picture is one extra-big piece of cardboard with long strips of cardboard zigzagging down the front of it. You know, so the marble runs along to the end of one strip, drops off the end onto the next strip, then repeats that all the way down until it reaches the bottom.'

'That's what I was thinking too,' I said. 'Sort of long chutes like this.' I borrowed the pencil from Cleo and squinted hard at the paper to draw a picture of what Bee had described. Without my glasses it was really hard to do anything accurately.

Cleo nodded. 'And do you think we should be trying to make the chutes for it to run down so that they're folded like a V, or so they have a flat base like a U?'

'Why don't we test it out?' I said, grabbing one of our pieces of cardboard and cutting two long strips. Bee folded one of them in half longways to make a V, whilst I struggled to fold the thick cardboard into a square U shape.

'The cardboard is pretty tough to fold,' I said,

holding up my strip. Instead of a U shape with two straight sides and a flat bottom, it was all squashed and mangled.

Bee nodded. Hers looked better than mine, but she still had trouble folding it.

'I think we need to score it first,' said Cleo.

'Oh,' said Bee, with a grin. 'Well then, I give mine a score of 3 out of 10.'

'Not *give it* a score,' said Cleo, laughing and rolling her eyes. 'I mean, *score it*. You know,

when you use the scissors to sort of mark the cardboard first before we try to fold it. That should help to make it straighter. Like this.'

She carefully took the scissors and closed them. Then she held her ruler onto the cardboard and ruled along the side of the ruler using the tip of the closed scissors. This made a dent in the cardboard, but it didn't cut through it. When I tried folding along the line she'd scored, it was so much easier and stayed super straight.

'So how long does it take a marble to run along a chute this long?' I asked. 'Because then we can just multiply it out to see how many folded strips we'll need to make for it to run along.'

'Let's test it,' said Bee. She held one end of her strip and sat the other end on the table. Cleo held the stopwatch, and when Bee released the marble at the top of her strip, she recorded the time using the stopwatch.

'That was about 0.5 seconds,' said Cleo. 'Let's do it again to double-check.'

Bee put down the strip, retrieved the marble and reset it at the top of the run. When Cleo clicked the stopwatch as the marble rolled onto the table at the end of the run, she frowned. 'That time was 0.7 seconds,' she said. 'Once more?'

They repeated the run three more times, each time with a different result.

'How are we supposed to create a long run that is exactly eight seconds?' complained Cleo.

'We can't even create a short run that has a consistent accurate time.'

'Do it a few more times,' I said.

Bee picked up the strip once more, positioned the marble at the top and let it run down, while Cleo clicked the stopwatch. I watched them perform each step carefully and by the third time, even without my glasses on, it was obvious what the problem was.

'You need to find something to rest the strip on,' I said to Bee. 'Each time you're holding it at a different height, so sometimes it's steeper and that makes the marble run faster.'

'Of course!' said Bee. 'So obvious now you mention it. What should I put it on?'

'Something low and flat,' I said. 'The slower times were when you were holding the strip almost flat on the table, with just a slight lift at one end to create the slope.'

We tried resting the strip on her pencil case and on some exercise books, but because it was a V shape, it couldn't balance on the point of the V, so it kept tipping to one side.

'Let's try the U-shaped one instead,' suggested Cleo. 'I think the flat bottom will help it to stay upright.'

I balanced one end of the strip on two of Bee's exercise books and released the marble. As it ran down the strip of cardboard, it bounced

from side to side, hitting the upright sides of the U-shaped cardboard.

Cleo frowned. 'I think the fact that the marble is hitting the sides will be a problem. It'll hit the edges a different amount of times each run, which will make it faster or slower. This is hard!' She pushed her sketchbook away in frustration and slid her pencil back into its spot in her pencil case. 'This is too hard!'

As I watched the pencil slide into the pencil holder, it gave me an idea.

'We just need to make the run narrower,' I said. 'It just needs to be exactly the diameter of the marble, then it won't be able to bump from side to side. Look!'

'The diam-what?' said Bee.

'The diameter,' I said. 'It's the distance from one side of the marble to the other if you could go through the middle.'

I took out her ruler and measured how wide the marble was. It was a bit tricky to measure an object that kept rolling away. I couldn't get the exact diameter because I couldn't actually make my ruler go through the centre of the marble, but finally I managed to get a measurement that I thought would work. I laid another cardboard strip on the table and scored it again with the scissors to make the flat bottom section of the U only ever so slightly wider than the width of the marble. After I'd folded up the sides, I handed it to Bee.

'Let's try this version,' I said, positioning the strip on top of her books and the marble at the top. This time, there was no space for the marble to move from side to side, so it ran from the top to the bottom smoothly and consistently every time. Cleo, still in charge of clicking the stopwatch, was impressed.

'Right, so then our next step is to –'

Cleo was interrupted by Dr Mathers' timer going off to signal the end of the session.

'Okay, girls,' she called from the front of the room. 'Time to pack up. There's a plastic tub up the front for you to store any of your cardboard and equipment in. I'll be coming past to check your workspaces before you leave to make sure everything is being left tidy, ready for tomorrow's classes in here.'

It took us less than a minute to slide all of our cardboard strips, scissors, glue and tape into

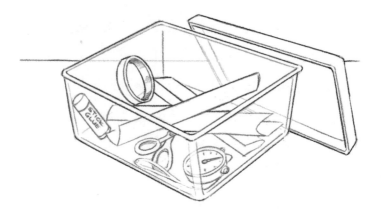

one of Dr Mathers' boxes. It felt like we hadn't actually got very far with our challenge at all. In fact, it looked like all we'd done for the last hour was to cut three strips of cardboard and folded them.

'It really looks like we haven't done a lot,' said Cleo, packing away the rest of our cardboard, along with our scissors and stopwatch. 'But, actually, I think we've learnt a lot this afternoon.'

I nodded. 'You're right. We've worked out that a flat bottom run will probably work better for us than a V shape, and also that it needs to be narrow enough that the marble can't bounce from one side of it to the other.'

'That's true,' said Bee. 'And we've learnt that we need to choose a set angle for the run to be on so that it always takes the same time.'

'It's great that we've found all of that out, but it means we still have a ton of work to do to be ready before next Thursday. We're definitely going to need the extra time in the Learning Lab on Monday,' said Cleo.

'How about we sit together at lunch tomorrow so we can talk more about our design?' said Bee, as we packed up our things at the end of the session. 'That way, we can have it all figured out and we can start construction during our lunch break on Monday.'

'Good idea,' said Cleo. She dropped her sketchbook and pencil into her school bag.

'Would that work for you, Alice?' asked Bee.

Would that work for me? Um, yes! Of course it would work for me. It would be amazing for me. Finally, some friends to sit with at lunch. I'd been so focused on our task today that I'd almost forgotten about having to keep being cool, new Alice. I'd been so focused on what we were doing with the marble run that I'd just been my normal self. I'll have to work extra hard at being cooler, otherwise Bee and Cleo won't want to be seen with me.

'Okay, sure. I think that'd be fine,' I replied, trying to act like it was no big deal, even though I was actually really excited.

Chapter Ten

I could hardly wait to sit with Bee and Cleo at lunchtime. It didn't even bother me that I had to survive our Friday PE session where we were practising hurdles. This wasn't my favourite activity, given that without my glasses I found it hard to judge how close to the hurdle I was until it was a bit too late. I spent most of the PE lesson tripping over hurdles and ending up flat on my face on the grass.

By the time I'd changed back into my school dress and grabbed my lunch bag, Bee and Cleo had already found a table outside the cafeteria. It was a long table with eight seats around it. They'd claimed places at one end, and there were three other girls sitting at the other. When they saw me coming, Bee stood up and gave a little wave to show me where they were. I smiled and waved back.

'Right,' said Cleo. 'I've been thinking about our marble run design so much since we left GAS yesterday. In fact, I feel like I may have even dreamt about it.'

Bee took a bite of her chicken sandwich and nodded vigorously as she chewed. 'Me too!' she said when she'd finally swallowed her mouthful. I was glad she wasn't having the cafeteria lunch. Today was meatball day, and I still had bad memories of the last time I was sitting across from someone in the cafeteria who was eating meatballs for lunch.

'I was thinking about our design and I drew this,' Cleo said. She pulled out one of her many sketchbooks to show us her idea. Cleo's such an amazing artist. Her marble run design was a big

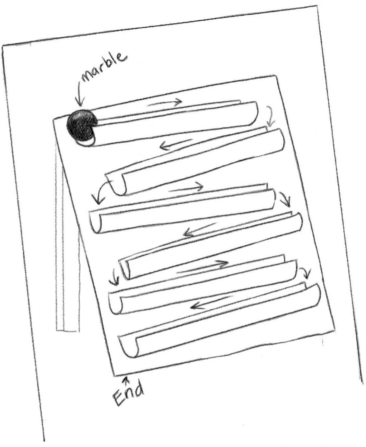

rectangular piece of cardboard with U-shaped strips running back and forth all of the way from the top to the bottom. She'd even drawn in some legs on the back of the piece of cardboard so that it could stand up by itself. The drawing was precise and coloured in using watercolour paints. I was excited. If her design was this good, imagine how good the real thing would be.

'I like the legs on the back of it,' I said. 'It'll stand up by itself and keep the angle exactly the same every time, just like when we did those test runs earlier.'

'That looks really good,' said Bee. 'We could definitely make it in the time that we have left.'

I nodded. 'And if we make all of the strips the same size, then we'll just have to trim the last one to try and get the time as close to eight seconds as possible.'

'Hey! Look who it is!' said a voice from the other end of the table.

I looked up and saw that Gigi, Darcy and Chelsie were the three girls who were sitting at the other end of the table. It was really a surprise because I'd been so focused on the marble run and enjoying lunch with Bee and Cleo that I hadn't even stopped to look around me. Also, I realised that I'd been so engrossed in what we were doing in GAS that I hadn't really thought about Gigi and our friendship in ages.

'What are you doing, Alice?' said Gigi.

I felt my face flush red. 'We're drawing some marble run designs for a challenge we're doing in GAS.'

'GAS?' said Gigi.

'Eww!' said Chelsie. 'That's so gross.' The three girls giggled.

'No, not *gas*,' Cleo said. 'It's G-A-S. It's short for Girls Achieving in STEM.'

'What's a stem?' asked Darcy.

'It's an acronym,' Bee said. 'It's short for –'

'An acro-what?' said Chelsie.

'And what are you drawing?' Darcy reached over and grabbed the sketchbook.

'Hey!' Bee said. 'Give that back.'

Darcy looked at the picture. 'What's it even meant to be?'

'It's our marble run,' Cleo said, grabbing at the sketchbook. 'You put a marble in at the top, and it runs down all of the little chutes until it reaches the bottom.'

'That's so dumb,' said Darcy. 'And why would you even want to make that, Alice?'

I'd been fiddling with my mermaid necklace between my fingers and trying to stay out of the conversation. I could still very clearly remember the meatball incident and I did not want to get into another argument in the cafeteria.

But now, I was thrust into the spotlight and, even worse than that, I was torn about how to respond. Part of me wanted to act all cool in front of Gigi and her friends, and the other part of me wanted to stand up for GAS and my new friendships.

And even though they were being mean, there was still a part of me that wanted Gigi and her new friends to like me. It sounds silly, I know, but it's true. And as I ran my fingers along the edges of the tiny mermaid around my neck, I was reminded of all of the fun times Gigi and I had spent together. I know, I know. It is not an excuse, but it kind of explains what happened next.

'Well... it is kind of dumb,' I agreed. 'I have no idea why anyone would want to spend their time making a marble run or even going to GAS. It's so stupid.' I tossed my ponytail back over my shoulder and glanced at the sketchbook like it was the most boring thing I'd ever seen.

Bee and Cleo both looked at me like I'd gone crazy.

'If you think it's so stupid, then why keep it?' said Gigi. She reached forward and tore the page with our marble run design right out of Cleo's sketchbook. 'Here you go, Alice. You can do the honours. Rip it up!'

'Yeah, rip it up,' said Darcy. All eyes were on me as Gigi handed me the page from the sketchbook. I looked at Bee and Cleo. I looked at Chelsie and Darcy. I looked at Gigi and just for a moment, I found myself imagining what it would be like if we were best friends again. I could remember all of the giggles in class together at our old school. All of the birthday parties we'd been to together. All of the sleepovers we'd had.

Could we go back to the good old days? Was this just a test to see if I was ready to be one of her friends again?

I took a deep breath, then I ripped the page in half and in half again and in half again until it was just a handful of tiny squares of paper.

Everyone at the table stared at me. There were looks of disbelief on their faces.

Cleo burst into tears. She jumped up and ran from the cafeteria.

'Alice! We were meant to be a team!' said Bee, grabbing her lunch bag and following Cleo out the door.

There was silence at the table.

Finally, it was broken by Gigi.

'Wow! I can't believe you actually did that,' she said. 'That was a really good drawing.'

'Yeah, I was just messing around,' said Chelsie.

'And I thought you guys were friends,' said Darcy.

At that moment, my form teacher, Miss Walker, who was picking up her lunch from the cafeteria, must have seen the commotion. 'Is everything okay here, girls?' she asked.

'It's fine,' said Chelsie. 'We were just leaving, weren't we, Gigi? Darcy?' The other two nodded, then they got up and walked off together, leaving me sitting at the table by myself, holding the tiny scraps of Cleo's design in my hands.

As I looked down at the ripped pieces, I realised that I'd made a bad choice. A really, really bad choice. I thought I'd impress Gigi and her new friends by ripping up the drawing, and that she would want me back as a best friend. Instead, she couldn't have cared less about the drawing, and I had upset Bee and Cleo. My actual friends. And if Gigi was my true friend, she'd never have asked me to do that to Cleo's picture.

For the first time all term, even without my glasses on, I could see things clearly. And I could see that I'd made a terrible mistake.

I felt my eyes filling with tears. It suddenly seemed like everyone in the cafeteria was staring at me, quietly crying at a table all alone, holding two handfuls of torn up paper. I stuffed the handfuls of paper into my pocket, grabbed my lunch bag and headed for the one place I knew was a safe place at St Mildred's.

The door to the Learning Lab was unlocked, so I let myself in and headed straight for our usual spot at the back. I dumped my lunch bag onto the table, put my head down on my arms and cried warm, wet tears. Everything at St Mildred's was ruined. I'd thrown away the opportunity to have the one thing I really wanted: friends. And worse than that, they were friends that I wanted. We liked the same things. We got on well together. They were true friends.

'Alice? I thought I heard the door open. What are you doing here?'

I lifted my head and saw Dr Mathers. She held

a box of tissues out to me. I pulled two out and dabbed at my eyes, then decided it would probably be better if I just took the whole box.

'Dr Mathers,' I said, wiping my eyes. 'I think I should drop out of GAS.'

Dr Mathers looked surprised. 'Why do you want to drop out, Alice?'

'It just isn't really going that well. I joined GAS because I needed to make some new friends at St Mildred's. And then I made some friends, but I didn't realise that I had. Then Bee and Cleo and I sort of got into a fight... well, not really a fight. It was me. I did something not very nice. Now they're mad with me, it's all a big mess and I think I should just quit GAS.'

'What did you do exactly, Alice?' said Dr Mathers.

I unzipped my pocket and dropped the pieces of Cleo's marble run design onto the table in front of Dr Mathers.

'Oh,' she said. 'I can see why they'd be upset with you.'

I sighed. 'I thought that to make friends here at St Mildred's I'd have to change who I am. I was trying to be the coolest girl at St Mildred's, but instead, now I feel like I've become the opposite. I've tried everything to make friends here and nothing has worked.'

I looked at Dr Mathers expectantly, hoping she'd give me the solution to my problem and a way to make it up to Cleo and Bee. Instead, she smiled and stepped back. Her glitter glasses frames caught the light and twinkled as she spoke.

'Well, I've seen you working on the challenges here at GAS. You're clever, Alice, and a good problem-solver. You've been practising that all term here at GAS. I'm sure you'll come up with a solution to this problem too.' She turned to head back to her office. 'I'll leave you to it. Just pop the box of tissues back on the shelf by the door when you go.'

I looked at Dr Mathers. 'Before you go, can I ask you something?'

I wiped away another tear with the back of my hand.

Dr Mathers nodded.

'How do you do it?' I asked. 'How can you be so cool *and* also wear glasses and love science, maths, engineering and technology too? Those things don't always go together.'

Dr Mathers laughed. 'There are two answers to that, Alice. Firstly, I'm just myself. I like what I like and if that makes me cool, so be it. The second answer is that if in doubt, some glitter makes everything cooler. Like my glasses – I just added the glitter myself.'

'Wait... you added that yourself? Can you show me how to do it?' The words were out of my mouth before I could stop myself.

'I definitely can help you with that,' she said

with a smile. 'But you'll need to work out how to make it up to Bee and Cleo by yourself. You're going to have to put in some effort to get them back.'

I nodded. She was right. I was going to have to come up with a seriously good idea over the weekend to repair the damage I'd done to my friendship with Bee and Cleo.

'And besides, you're the only Year 5 team that is even close to winning a spot at the Think League Challenge at this stage, and it would be great to not have only Year 8 teams representing us. Don't you think?'

'I'll do my best,' I said.

Dr Mathers smiled, 'I know you will, Alice. Now, let me introduce you to my top-secret collection of glitter nail polish that will transform your glasses into the coolest pair of frames around!'

Chapter Eleven

Over the weekend, I had lots of time to admire my new, red glitter glasses in the mirror. Dr Mathers had shown me how to pop the lenses out, and we carefully painted the red frames with a nail polish that had zillions of tiny flecks of silver glitter in it. Once the polish had dried, she just popped my lenses back into position and voilà! My glasses now had cool glitter frames.

I also had a lot of time to think about what had happened at lunchtime on Friday with Bee and Cleo. I thought back to Chinese New Year when I'd written my wishes onto the special paper and released them into the sky. *I want to be popular. I want to have friends.* Thinking about everything that had happened at lunchtime on

Friday, it was now clear to me: being popular and having friends are actually two very different things. And I know which one is more important. I'd much rather have friends than to be one of the so-called 'popular girls'. And I'd like those friends to be Bee and Cleo.

But what would I have to do to win them back?

I wasn't exactly sure what it would take, but by Sunday afternoon, I'd come up with a plan. But there was no way I could make it happen all by myself. I knew I had to ask for help and I knew just who to ask.

Mum was sitting at one end of the kitchen table, surrounded by piles of patient files. She was adding notes to different pages and typing things in on her computer.

'Hey, Mum,' I said, pulling up a chair next to her. 'I was wondering if you could help me with something.'

'Mmmm,' said Mum. Her eyes barely left the computer screen.

'Mum!' I said again. 'Mum!'

Even when she was at home, when Mum was in work mode, it could be really hard to get her attention.

'Yes, Alice?' she said, turning to the next patient file and continuing to type.

When Mum kept working away, I could feel myself getting cross, even though I didn't want to be.

'Mum, I need your help!' I said, then I dumped the pile of torn paper that made up Cleo's design

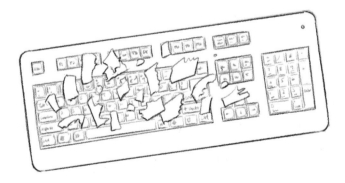

onto the keyboard in front of her. All of the little pieces of paper fluttered over her hands like snowflakes. Mum looked up in surprise.

'What's all this, Alice?' She finally stopped what she was doing and looked up.

I folded my arms across my chest. 'It's a big mess. That's what it is,' I snapped at her. My face felt all hot and, despite my best efforts, I could feel tears coming on.

'I can see that,' said Mum. 'There's no need to get all worked up about it, Alice.'

I rolled my eyes. 'Well, it feels like sometimes I won't get your attention unless I get all upset. You're always busy with your work.'

'Being a neurosurgeon is a very important job, Alice. My patients need me to look after them.'

'And being a mum is also an important job!' I said. 'I need you to look after me sometimes too.'

Mum looked at me for a moment, then she

closed the file in front of her. 'You know what? You're right, Alice. They're both important jobs.'

'They are,' I replied. 'I just feel like it's very hard to get your attention as a mum, but not as a brain surgeon.'

Mum nodded slowly. 'I just enjoy my work so much that I want to keep working, even when I'm at home. I think we should make a deal. *I'll* try to do less work at home, if *you* try to not get all grumpy while you're trying to get my attention when you need it.'

She held out her little finger. 'Pinkie promise?'

I tucked my pinkie finger around hers and together we shook. 'Pinkie promise.'

'Right,' she said, suddenly businesslike. 'Now, tell me about what's going on with all of these little pieces of paper.'

I wasn't quite sure exactly where to start, so I told her about how things had been hard at

St Mildred's, and about how Gigi hadn't been a great friend. Then I told her all about GAS and Bee and Cleo and the Think League Challenge and how I'd made a really big mistake. That part was the hardest because I had to admit that I hadn't been a great friend either.

'And so now, I need your help to put the picture back together so I can try and make things up to Bee and Cleo,' I finished. Because she operates on people's brains, Mum has very steady hands and I knew she'd be able to help me.

Mum slid her glasses down her nose and inspected the pile of paper, then nodded. 'I definitely think I can help. We're going to need tissue paper, PVA glue and a brush. I think I have the rest of the tools we might need in my briefcase.' I ran off to get everything she'd requested, and when I came back downstairs, she'd cleared off her files and had set up a mini-surgery. She'd even grabbed her pair of medical tweezers to help her to carefully hold each torn up piece.

'Right, now we're ready to start. Scalpel?' she said. She held out her hand.

'Mum, there is no scalpel. This isn't a proper surgery!' I said.

Mum chuckled to herself. 'I know, Alice. I was just being silly. But I *am* going to need an assistant. Where's Dorothy?'

Mum set Dorothy up on a chair alongside her. It was going to be Dorothy's job to organise all of the pieces into the correct order before they began sticking them down. It was like working on a jigsaw puzzle. Once work was underway on repairing the picture, I set about organising the next part of my plan. This part involved getting Nai Nai connected to the Internet.

'Nai Nai,' I said, giving my grandmother a hug and sitting down next to her on the couch. 'I really like the way you've been plaiting my hair all of these years, but... well, I think I've grown out of that style a bit, now that I'm in Year 5. Do you think you could learn how to do some of these hairstyles for me?' I asked. I gave her my laptop and clicked on one of the how-to videos that I'd found. The videos were all in English, but Nai Nai could understand what they were doing just by watching them, and we had fun together

trying them out on my hair. When Dorothy was
finished helping Mum, Nai Nai did a cute bun in
her hair. She also did a side braid in Mum's hair
whilst she was using her tweezers to gently stick
the final pieces of the picture onto the tissue
paper backing. Then Nai Nai even went into the
kitchen and offered to style Dad's hair for him
in one of the new ways that she'd learnt, but he
laughed and batted her away.

After Nai Nai had agreed to do a Chinese

ladder braid in my hair for school the next day, we left Cleo's design to dry on the kitchen table overnight. I was ready to try to make it up to Bee and Cleo. I just had to get past the hardest part: apologising to them.

When it came to lunchtime on Monday, the Learning Lab was packed with girls from GAS all working on their marble runs. The room was buzzing with conversation and the sound of marbles rolling back and forth on pieces of cardboard.

Dr Mathers was talking to some Year 12 girls about their science classwork at the front of the room. She gave me a thumbs-up as I came in. I gave her a little wave back. Bee and Cleo were working together up the back.

'It just isn't right,' said Cleo. She dropped the marble into the top of the run and watched as it whizzed back and forth down the chutes they'd made and dropped into her hand at the end. 'It just goes too quickly,' she said. 'It needs to be about one and a half seconds slower.'

'I know,' Bee replied, frowning. 'But if we make the cardboard backboard any taller, it won't be able to stand up by itself. And we can't fit any extra strips in for the marble to run down.'

They stopped talking when they saw me coming. Cleo turned to face me, arms crossed and her body protectively positioned between me and the marble run.

I took a deep breath.

'I'm really sorry about Friday,' I said. 'You know, with the paper and stuff.'

Cleo glared at me. For someone so tiny, she really looked fierce.

'I should have stood up for you instead of trying to impress Gigi and her friends,' I continued. 'I... I... well, I made a bad choice.'

Bee nodded. 'You can say *that* again.'

Cleo just pursed her lips, so I added. 'I know I haven't always been easy to have in your group. And... what I'm trying to say is that you don't have to be friends with me right now, but I'm hoping that maybe one day we can be. I'm ready to be the best team member ever... if you still want me on the team... maybe?'

Bee and Cleo looked at each other, then back at me.

'How do we know you aren't just going to ditch us again when you get the chance?' Cleo said.

'I promise I'm not the person that I've been pretending to be. I promise I'm just me. Look, I'm wearing my glasses now, and my grandmother did my hair for me. No more walking around bumping into things and no more trying to style my hair all messy like the girls in the magazines.'

Cleo was still suspicious.

To show how serious I was, I unclasped the mermaid necklace from around my neck. It had been a symbol of my friendship with Gigi, but now that was definitely finished. The mermaid charm glinted in the sun, and I admired it one last time. Then I opened my hand and let it drop into the rubbish bin. Bee let out a little gasp.

'See? I swear I'm willing to do whatever it takes to make it up to you both.'

Cleo still looked a little dubious. 'Whatever it takes?'

I carefully reached into my pocket and pulled out Cleo's drawing that Mum had carefully glued back together for me. It wasn't the same as it used to be, but Mum had done a very precise job of putting it back together.

I handed it to Cleo. 'It isn't exactly the same as the original copy, but Mum and my sister, Dorothy, managed to get all the pieces put back where they belong.'

Cleo took the drawing. It was more delicate now, but also quite beautiful with the tissue paper backing Mum had used to keep the pieces together. '*Original copy*,' she murmured. 'That's an oxymoron, you know.'

'Actually, *that* I *do* know,' I smiled. 'Oxymorons are my favourites!' There was a long, awkward pause as the three of us looked at each other.

'So... am I forgiven?' I asked.

Cleo spoke first. 'All of these things are great,' she said. 'But do you promise not to dump us again to try to be friends with someone you think might be cooler?'

I nodded and held up my hand like a girl guide

making a pledge. 'I promise to be myself, just Alice, always.'

Bee smiled. 'And I have a question too. Is there something you can think of to help us to slow down our marble run?'

I think it was walking around looking after a pile of ripped up paper for three days that made me think of it. The answer just came to me.

'I think we need to rip up the cardboard.'

'What?' yelped Cleo, holding on to her freshly repaired drawing. 'Surely it's too soon to be suggesting we rip up anything?'

I smiled. 'The cardboard. Look at this piece. See how it's smooth on the top and the bottom, but there's sort of a zigzag layer in between.'

I grabbed one of the offcut pieces of cardboard from the table and peeled off the top smooth layer of cardboard to reveal the bumpy surface underneath.

'This is corrugated cardboard. They put this zigzag layer in between the two smooth pieces of cardboard like a sandwich, and it makes the cardboard really strong. If we peel back the top layer of cardboard, we can run the marble down the corrugated part and the friction will slow it down.'

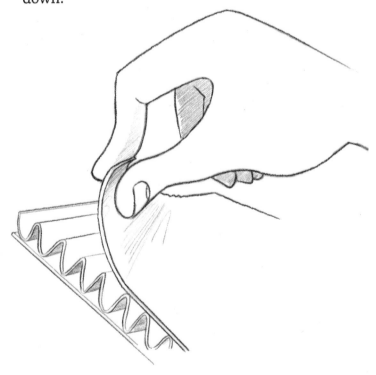

'Seriously, Alice,' said Cleo. 'I really want to be still a little bit cross with you right now, but that idea is pretty good and I just can't stay mad. I actually think you're onto something.'

'Let's peel the top layers off the chutes on our run and see if we can make a difference to our time. Start with the first chute. We can do it one at a time, then test it with the marble to see how it changes the timing. Ready, Alice?'

I pushed my glasses back up the bridge of my nose and flipped my braid over my shoulder. 'Ready!'

Chapter Twelve

'I can't even look,' I exclaimed. My eyes were squeezed tight.

'It's going to be a long afternoon if you don't look,' said Bee. She elbowed me in the side. 'You've got your glasses on now; you might as well use them to actually see things.'

I smiled and opened my eyes. Everyone at GAS was sitting on chairs arranged in a semi-circle several rows deep. At the front, there were seven marble runs lined up on a couple of tables that had been pushed together. The atmosphere in the room was a mixture of excitement and nervousness as today was the day that would decide which teams would progress through to represent GAS at the Think League Challenge.

'Come on, Dr Mathers,' said Chayla, one of the Year 8 girls. 'Can we start now?'

Melody clearly agreed. 'We need to get started immediately. I cannot stand the suspense any longer.'

Dr Mathers, in a cheerful, red and blue, striped jumper, raised her hand to get everyone's attention. 'Before we begin, let's just check the scoreboard.' She pointed to the whiteboard behind her. 'As you can see, there are five teams that are very close and any of them could win, given that today's challenge is worth 8 points. If your marble run takes exactly eight seconds, you will get all of your points. For every millisecond that your marble run is over or under, you will lose that many points.'

Everyone was silent for a moment, then one of the Year 7 piped up. 'Hang on, so if our time is, say, I don't know. Something like 8.52. Then we'll lose 52 points?'

Dr Mathers nodded. 'So you'll take 8 away from 52, which will give you 44. Then you'll subtract 44 from your current score.'

'That means anyone could win,' said Chayla. A murmur went through the crowd.

Another oxymoron crossed my mind. 'That's *even odds*,' I thought.

'And, actually, that means some teams might even end up with a minus or negative score on the board,' continued Chayla. Was she right?

'That's correct,' said Dr Mathers. 'It all comes down to how precise you've been whilst making your marble run. Shall we get started then?'

Looking at the marble runs, it was actually surprising how different they each were.

Melody's group were the first to go. They'd come up with a marble run that was made from one long chute that curled around and

around like a water slide, with cardboard rolls underneath to hold it up. There were a lot of curves and corners that had been carefully joined together to create it.

'I wish I was as small as a marble because that looks like it would be the most fun slide to go down,' whispered Cleo.

Bee giggled. 'I kind of agree with you.'

Melody positioned the marble at the top, and Dr Mathers started the stopwatch the moment she let it go. The marble rolled down the run so smoothly and landed at the bottom almost exactly on time.

'8.04 seconds!' announced Dr Mathers, and all of the waiting teams cheered.

'They're going to be hard to beat. I think they've got a spot in the top three for sure,' I said. Bee and Cleo both nodded.

The next two teams had a few problems with their designs. They were similar to ours in that they were straight back and forth. But one group used the V-shaped strips of cardboard instead of having a flat, U-shaped run and their marble dropped off the edge at one point halfway down the run. The other group didn't have a stand on the back, so one of the group members had to hold it up and, as we found when we were testing ours, just the slightest change of angle could really impact how fast or slow your marble would roll. They must have held theirs up too steeply because their marble hit the bottom in around seven seconds.

The fourth group was made up of Chayla, Enid and Aiden, all from Year 8. They were also a shoo-in to get a spot at the Think League Challenge, and it was easy to see why with their marble run. It was the only one that included a loop-the-loop section, just like a roller coaster, and a trap door where it looked like the marble was going to keep going, but instead dropped through the secret door and reappeared in a different spot! It was both impressive to watch and accurate, gaining them a time of 8.12 seconds.

'These Year 8 teams are doing so well,' said Bee. 'There's no way we're going to get through.'

'That's okay,' I said. 'They've had a lot more experience than us. Plus I know I've learnt a lot of other things along the way with this challenge too.'

'That's true,' said Bee. 'But I'd still like to win. It would be so good to go home and tell my brothers that I get to go to the Think League Challenge this year.'

The team after the Year 8s who'd had the loop-the-loop design were a bit too slow with a time of over nine seconds. The sixth team had used some rough cardboard surfaces to provide friction, just like our marble run, and they had the most accurate time so far. When Dr Mathers stopped the timer at 8.02 seconds, the crowd went wild. That was one of the nice things about GAS, I realised. Even though we were competing against each other, everyone was always happy for everyone else when they succeeded.

Finally, it was our turn. I scrunched my eyes tightly closed and took a deep breath.

'Alice, seriously! Open your eyes. You'll miss our turn!' Bee elbowed me in the side again.

'And if you trip over and squash our marble run, there will definitely be tears – yours and

mine, and probably some from Bee as well!'
added Cleo. We all giggled as we made our way
up to the front. Cleo took the marble from Dr
Mathers, while Bee and I stood either side of
our creation.

'I can hardly bear to watch,' mumbled Bee. I
nodded. Cleo held the marble at the top of the
run and made eye contact with Dr Mathers.

'Ready, go!' she said, and Cleo released the
marble.

Looking at the girls in the audience watching
our marble going back and forth down our
marble run was like looking at a crowd all
watching a tennis match. It was so quiet, and
you could see their heads going back and forth
as the marble ran along one cardboard chute and
dropped off the end, only to be caught by the
next folded cardboard chute underneath. It was
the most mesmerising eight seconds of my life.

Finally, the marble dropped off the end of the final chute and into Bee's waiting hand.

Dr Mathers clicked her stopwatch and smiled. 'That was 8.07 seconds,' she said.

The girls in the audience clapped and cheered for us, just like they'd done with the other groups, but I couldn't help but feel disappointed: 8.07 seconds. There were other groups that were much more accurate than us, and that meant that we weren't going to be one of the teams going to the Think League Challenge. It seemed funny to me at that moment that I was disappointed. Up until this week, I hadn't really given the Think League Challenge much thought. I'd been too busy worrying about what everyone else thought about me to worry about what might happen if we won a spot as one of the teams that would get to go. But now that I'd been working together with Bee and Cleo on our marble run, I really, really wanted to go. And it appeared that I wasn't the only one. The cheering had died down and now there was a different sound filling the room. It was one of discussion.

'Can someone read me out the scores from the board?' asked Enid. She had all of the times from all of the teams written down and she was frantically calculating to work out which teams had made it through.

Then I remembered. It wasn't just the most accurate marble run today; it was the best score overall. So our marble run time was 8.07 seconds. The extra 0.07 seconds were a penalty for us, so we had to subtract 7 from 8, which gave us a total of 1 point to add to our total. There wasn't much separating the top five teams in the competition, so it was going to be close!

'Okay, I think we've worked it out. I did all of the adding and subtracting, and Aiden double-checked it for me. This is what we think, Dr Mathers.' She handed her pad of paper to Dr Mathers, who checked it against her own working out, then nodded.

'The three teams we'll be taking with us to the Think League Challenge are... drum roll, please.' The girls began to patter their hands on their legs enthusiastically.

'First it's Melody, Kate and Lauren, then it's Chayla, Enid and Aiden, and finally we'll be taking Alice, Bee and Cleo.'

Us? We get to go? Before I had any more time to think about it, I was squeezed into a hug sandwich between Bee and Cleo.

'Yes!' exclaimed Cleo. For someone so tiny, she really was extremely loud. Bee, on the other hand, had a couple of tears running down her cheeks.

'Well done,' I said to both of them. 'You both worked super hard to get our marble run just right.'

Bee smiled. 'Well, even though we've had our ups and downs as a team, we definitely couldn't have done it without you, Alice.'

The celebrations would have continued all afternoon if Dr Mathers had let them. Even the teams that weren't selected were having a great time, cheerfully testing out the marble runs of other teams and commiserating about what went wrong with their own designs. Finally, it was time to pack it all up.

'Now the best thing about our marble runs being made from old cardboard boxes is that they can easily be recycled. If you don't want to keep your marble run to take home, please take it apart and drop the pieces into the recycling bin on your way out. And could I see the winning teams for a moment before you go, please?' said Dr Mathers.

We clustered around Dr Mathers to hear what she had to say. 'Girls, I need to put in our Think League Challenge entries tomorrow. Can you please let me know first thing in the morning what team name you'd like to be entered under? Unless, of course, you want to be called GAS 1, GAS 2 and GAS 3?'

All of the groups laughed. I was used to the group GAS now, but it still wasn't a name that I was very keen on. I mean, it doesn't matter how fun the group is, nobody wants to say to their friends that they can't hang out after school because they've got GAS.

Bee, Cleo and I dropped our marble run into the recycling bin and grabbed our school bags from outside the Learning Lab. As we walked, I opened my lunch box and shared one of Dad's latest creations, dulce de nian gao, with my friends. He'd decided to branch out into desserts and had spent the weekend perfecting a Mexican-inspired version of this delicious Chinese dessert made of a brown sugar cake wrapped in pastry. He'd added the sweet caramel of dulce de leche from Latin America and had deep fried it just like nian gao from China.

'What should we be called?' said Cleo, taking a huge bite of her piece of nian gao. 'This is so yum!'

'I don't think we should be called that!' I laughed. 'My vote is for anything, except GAS. It's just not the coolest name for this group.'

Bee rolled her eyes and licked the caramel off her fingers. 'But I thought you didn't care about being cool any more, Alice.'

I flushed. 'I mean, I really don't. I just don't think it's going to be that great going to the Think League Challenge being called GAS. Can't we think of something that's even a little bit better?'

Cleo laughed. 'I think you're totally right. What name were you thinking we should use instead?'

'I hadn't got that far,' I shrugged. 'All I'd decided was that GAS wasn't great!'

Bee, Cleo and I were so busy chatting and eating that we barely noticed Gigi, Chelsie and Darcy walking across the far side of the Quad. They had wet hair, so I'm guessing they'd just finished after-school diving. Out of the corner of my eye, I saw Gigi watching us. Like properly staring. It was like she couldn't believe we were still friends, even after the ripping up incident in the cafeteria.

What came next seemed to happen in slow motion. Gigi was so busy watching us chatting and laughing together that she didn't watch where she was going.

She ploughed straight into a rubbish bin.

Both Gigi and the bin fell over. Rubbish and

food scraps flew everywhere, covering her school
dress. I stifled a giggle. The whole thing looked
pretty funny. But wait a minute! What's this?

Gigi grabbing something that had fallen out of her pocket during the fall! It was her Winnie Mermini necklace! She'd kept it after all! So, perhaps she wasn't as cool as she was trying to make herself out to be!

While Gigi scrambled around on the ground, trying to get out of the rubbish and adjust her dress, Darcy and Chelsie screwed up their noses at the smell, laughed at her and walked further away across the Quad instead of helping her up.

It made me wonder if they were really her true friends after all, but I guess that was something for her to worry about. Trying to be best friends with Gigi was no longer a problem for me, and that felt really good.

Bee, Cleo and I finished off the last of our nian gao as we passed under the sandstone archway and headed down the driveway.

'What about SCFG?' suggested Bee, bringing

me back to the group name conversation. 'It could be short for STEM Club for Girls.'

'It might be hard to remember all of those letters in the right order. What about just STEM Girls?' said Cleo.

'The only problem with that is that I didn't know what STEM was when I first joined. Mrs Barry in the Office had to explain to me what each of the letters stood for.' I cringed at the memory.

'How about The Clever Cookies? Or The Bright Ideas?' said Bee.

'The Brainiacs? Hmm, maybe too nerdy?' said Cleo.

'How about The Curiosity Club?' I said.

Cleo's eyes lit up with excitement. 'I love it!'

Bee nodded and tucked her hair behind her ears. 'It's perfect. I'll let Dr Mathers know in the morning.'

'I can sketch up some possible logo designs for us!' said Cleo. 'And we can meet at lunchtime tomorrow to discuss them. Maybe we could make team T-shirts or something? How does that sound?'

'Perfect!' said Bee. 'Alice?'

'Now that would definitely be cool. Very cool,' I smiled. 'Let's do it!'